GLEAMING BRIGHT

GLEAMING BRIGHT

Josepha Sherman

Walker and Company
New York

First published in the United States of America in 1994 by Walker
Publishing Company, Inc.

Published simultaneously in Canada by Thomas Allen & Son Canada,
Limited, Markham, Ontario

Library of Congress Cataloging-in-Publication Data
Sherman, Josepha.
Gleaming bright / Josepha Sherman.
p.   cm.
Summary: To avoid being married to a cruel king, and to save her
father's kingdom from ruin, a resourceful young princess goes in
search of the magic box that was stolen from her grandfather by an
evil wizard.
ISBN 0-8027-8296-5
[1. Fantasy.]   I. Title.
PZ7.S54575G1   1994
[Fic]—dc20   93-24156
CIP
AC

Printed in the United States of America

2   4   6   8   10   9   7   5   3   1

CONTENTS

PROLOGUE

THE SPRITE FLEW FRANTICALLY through the forest, a sleek little manlike form, its rainbow wings a blur, dodging branches, diving suddenly to flutter around and around the plainly clad old man seated on the tree stump and chittering at him in its high, thin little voice: "Coming, danger coming, enemy!"

The old man, Cathbad the wizard, held up a hand, and the sprite perched on it, weightless as a bird and shivering, still chittering, "Enemy! Enemy comes!"

"Who?" For all his impatience, Cathbad spoke gently. One had to be patient with sprites, or the near-mindless little things panicked and flew away. "Who is the enemy?"

"Rhegeth!" the sprite screamed, and took to the air with a flurry. Cathbad got slowly to his feet, ignoring the protests of his ancient body, smoothing down his plain brown robe with steady hands.

You never will learn, will you, Rhegeth?

He stood quietly, cloaking himself in shadow and wizardry, as the other, younger wizard approached as warily as any stalking predator. Cathbad looked at the black robe, black cloak, black hood half-hiding the strong, sharp-featured young face, and shook his head. Rhegeth always did have a taste for the overly dramatic.

"That's far enough," Cathbad said.

Rhegeth started, whirling, hand raised to gesture, magic glittering about his fingers.

"Don't," the older wizard snapped. "I may be a hundred years and more your senior, but you still haven't the strength or skill to stand against me, and we both know it."

With an angry hiss, the other lowered his hand.

"That's better. You're trespassing, Rhegeth. Go."

But Rhegeth was staring at him with a sudden fierce intensity. Cathbad locked his cool blue gaze with that hot black glare. Power crackled in the air between them, and a wind began to swirl about them, stirring Cathbad's white hair and mustache, making Rhegeth's black cloak flutter like the wings of a great bird. Neither wizard moved as the tension of magic against magic grew with the wind. Cathbad was dimly aware of his heart pounding, of the blood surging in his ears. In another moment he would have to yield, and then . . .

But Rhegeth broke first. With a gasp of exhaustion, he gave way, staggering back under the weight of Cathbad's suddenly released magic. The older wizard let him feel the full force of Power crushing him to the ground, then drew it back into himself. Rhegeth lay still for a time, chest heaving with the force of his panting. Then he struggled back to his feet. Without a word to

Cathbad, he threw his black cloak about him with a dramatic swirl and stalked away. Cathbad, not trusting him for a moment, stood watch, rigidly alert, till the last trace of the younger wizard's aura was gone. Only then did he let himself sink to a rock with a shaken sigh. The rainbow-winged sprite darted down to land on his shoulder, twittering anxiously, and Cathbad stroked its sleek blue hair with a gentle finger.

"I'm getting too old for this, little one. And one of these days Rhegeth is going to figure that out. But, till then . . . Ah, curse it, how could I ever have made such a mistake? Why, oh why, did I ever teach him magic?"

❧

King Donal of Irwain, that small, forest-girded land, was young, high-spirited, and impulsive. And so it was no wonder that when he and his men went hunting, he had hurried ahead of them all. Donal was tall, dark of hair and neat new mustache, and startlingly blue of eye. Those eyes held just a trace of worry now, for Donal was quite lost, and without even a hunting horn to let the rest of his party find him again.

But before he could begin to worry in earnest, the young king heard a shout, a scuffle, an angry squeal that could only mean one thing: boar.

And a boar it was, Donal saw as he peered through the underbrush into a small clearing—or at least he *thought* it was a boar. It was bigger than any such had a right to be, its hide a dull, dead black, and its tusks glinted as sharply as curved knives. Its eyes were twin red flames.

Donal, very much aware that he had only two light javelins with him—spears meant to be thrown at smaller game—would have gladly stolen away before this monstrous thing could scent him. But to his horror, he saw that the boar had cornered a white-haired old man against a tree and was about to kill him.

At least I do have the javelins, Donal thought, and hurled the first. It struck the boar full in the side, and the monster whirled to him with a squeal of pain and rage. The fiery eyes blazed, and Donal thought, *Ah well, here's where I die,* but shouted defiantly, "Come on, you monster, come and die!"

It charged him. Donal threw his second and last javelin with all the strength within him—

And it pierced the boar through one terrible eye to the brain. In the next moment the monster, already dead, was upon him. Donal twisted desperately aside as the boar fell, crying out in pain as one gleaming tusk tore his arm. Gasping, he struggled free of the boar's crushing weight and clutched the wound, trying to stanch the bleeding. Dimly he heard the old man hurry to his side. Cool hands, amazingly strong, pulled his own away, then pressed firmly down on his arm. The sickening pain vanished with the touch. The old man murmured something soft and intricate, face taut with strain, and Donal froze, transfixed by the power suddenly blazing in those ancient blue eyes.

But all at once the strangeness was gone. The old man let out his breath in a weary sigh, just like any other man, and drew his hands away, wiping them clean on a scrap of cloth Donal could have sworn he'd pulled from the air, and commenting calmly: "I'm afraid that tunic is ruined."

The young king glanced nervously down at his arm and gasped anew. Where a jagged gash should be was only the thin white line of a healed wound.

"You're a wizard," he said, almost accusingly, and the old man laughed.

"The wizard Cathbad, to be precise. And you would be, I think, King Donal of Irwain."

"Uh, yes." Donal shook his head to clear it, telling himself that *of course* a wizard would know who he was without needing to be told. "I don't understand. If you're a wizard, why didn't you just—"

"Use my powers on that thing? The boar was created by . . . shall we say . . . a rival. Rhegeth. He made it immune to any magic but his own—as I nearly learned to my cost. Young Donal, you saved my life. Permit the wizard Cathbad to show you his gratitude."

"Oh, no need—"

"Hush. Follow me."

He touched Donal's head, and the king's scattered strength returned. He scrambled up, hurrying after the wizard, who moved with a young man's speed and grace.

Was this a hut they'd reached? Or was it some- how something grander, a fine hall worthy of a lord? Donal blinked, blinked again at that shifting, confusing scene, unable to quite pierce the mist engulfing the wizard's home.

"Wait here," Cathbad said shortly, and van- ished, only to reappear so suddenly that Donal yelped in surprise. The wizard smiled. "A man so eager to risk his life for another surely cares more for his people's welfare than his own."

Donal felt his face redden. "Well, yes, but . . ."

"Here."

The king drew in his breath sharply in wonder. The lidded box he held was small, not much longer than his two hands together, and covered from lid to sides to bottom with intricate inter- laced designs that made him dizzy when he tried to follow their twistings with his gaze. The box was also surprisingly light, considering that every gorgeous bit of it was the brightest, most dazzling gold.

"This is a princely gift!"

"Oh, indeed." Amusement flickered in the wiz- ard's eyes. "And more. This is Gleaming Bright, a thing of magic from the Old Days."

"Magic! But—but it's so small. And so light! There can't possibly be anything inside it."

"There isn't. Not now." All at once Cathbad's face was deadly serious. "Gleaming Bright is a granter of wishes, King Donal—oh, don't stare like that! I haven't given you the way to endless riches! Gleaming Bright will grant wishes only for you or one of your direct line—and only then if the magic itself agrees the wisher's need is real. Remember that, King Donal: you cannot use it for frivolous ends. Gleaming Bright will only grant a wish when *it* chooses. And no mere mortal can guess how it will choose to answer. Use it rarely, King Donal. And use it wisely."

Donal looked down at the box with uneasy respect. "I will," he promised.

❧

No one noticed small, cunning Echi crouching there, oh no, not man, not wizard. Only the Master noticed Echi, sending it here, there at the Master's will. The little creature, not much bigger than a fox or a young human child, shivered, remembering cruel spells and beatings when obedience had not been quite enough.

But this time, this time, the Master would praise, not hurt. Echi shivered again, now with delight, wrapping long, thin, black-furred arms about its scrawny black-furred body, bright black eyes staring out of its wizened face in wonder at the most beautiful object ever, ever: the glittery golden thing the man held, the thing that shimmered with magic.

At last Echi managed to tear its gaze away. Surely the Master would want the beautiful golden glittery thing for his very own. And when Echi brought it to him, oh, the Master would be so pleased! There would be no more beatings for poor Echi, no, no; there would be warmth and good things to eat, and oh, at last there would be pettings.

Unfolding its lanky legs, Echi went scuttling silently off to the Master. To Rhegeth.

☙

The boy glanced fearfully over his shoulder, terrified that they might be coming after him. He had been alone for as far back as he could recall, struggling to survive in the village streets, thrown a scrap of charity here, a bit of abstract kindness there, learning envy, learning hate—oh, watching those pig-fat merchants munching sweetmeats while he lurked like a gaunt little shadow, belly aching with hunger, he'd learned to hate very well. There was wisdom for you: trust no one, love no one, believe no one. The lesson was driven home the day the foreign merchants came, those sleek, cold-eyed men who, the streetwise murmured, dealt in slaves as well as spices. The boy knew only too well what happened to children who fell into such predators' hands. And when they'd looked his way, he'd run, and was running still, all the way into the trackless, boundless forest, where none could find him. No one human. But the shadows all around were fearsome things, and who knew what horrors lay behind them? Wild things, demons, lurking, stalking, coming ever closer—

Rhegeth awoke with a start, stifling a curse. He'd come so far since those terrible days. Why should such weak, useless memories still haunt him?

He rose, standing stock still as a voiceless

shadow of a servant that had once been a man dressed him in his dramatic black, his mind still in the past, remembering how at last he'd been found not by a demon but by Cathbad. The wizard had seen the seeds of magic within the frantic boy and asked him, "Would you wield Power?"

Rhegeth snorted and pulled impatiently away from the servant, who instantly groveled. Ignoring the creature, the Dark Druid stalked silently down the empty halls of his keep. "Would you wield Power?" Bah, what fool wouldn't?

But once he'd agreed, there had come the long, tedious years of study, of training, of tasting just the smallest crumbs of that Power. Oh, Cathbad had guarded his secrets well! Pretending kindness, pretending sympathy—lies, all lies! Rhegeth knew that the old man had been lording it over his pupil, keeping him humble, telling the boy he was keeping the study of High Magic from him for his soul's sake, insisting Rhegeth must learn love, learn control, learn compassion—

Learn weakness!

He wasn't weak now, not after having left Cathbad and turning his back on the soft magics of Light. And if the path he'd chosen was lonely, if sometimes, deep in the night, he ached for the company of men, of women, for song and laughter and light, the Power he'd gained was worth it all.

A servant, one of the few he'd left with a voice, whispered that Echi had returned. Rhegeth entered his Great Hall, a quiet, shadowy place, and took his seat on the elegantly carved chair, the Master's chair. He listened to Echi, the small, cowering thing, without a trace of outer emotion. But Rhegeth's mind was racing.

Gleaming Bright. So much Power concentrated in one little artifact. That Cathbad had keyed the thing only to Donal and his line meant nothing; magic could always be twisted by any who possessed sufficient will.

As did he. Leaning forward in his chair, Rhegeth told Echi, voice carefully neutral, "Bring me this golden box."

The little creature bowed so low its tufted ears scraped the floor, then scurried away. Rhegeth stared after it, hands clenched on the arms of his ornate chair, hardly believing his good fortune. Oh yes, Cathbad had lorded it over him all these years. Cathbad was still able to lord it over him, as the latest humiliating defeat had proven. But the old man couldn't last forever. Echi was a skillful little thief, and terrified of failing its master. Soon Gleaming Bright would be here. And once Rhegeth added its strength to his own . . .

Sitting alone in shadow, in his silent, lonely hall, the Dark Druid smiled.

ONE

Finola

UNA, FORMERLY NURSE TO Princess Finola, now (since Finola, at sixteen, was too old for such things as nurses) her chief lady-servant, paused in the doorway to the king's house. Hands on her plump hips, the woman looked about the bare earth courtyard and the royal town beyond it, biting her lip in vexation. *Now* where was the girl?

All about her, the folk of Irwain-the-town in Irwain-the-land were going about their daily affairs, going in or coming out of their circular, thatched-roof homes, tunics, gowns, and woolen cloaks dyed in a rainbow of bright colors swirling about them, pausing to chat with friends or barter for pots, tools, or vegetables, safe within the town's high wooden palisade. One would almost think, mused Una, that there'd never been a drought this past year or a poor harvest; people did tend to live in the present.

But nowhere in all the bustle was there a sign of the princess herself. Una impatiently brushed a fat gray braid back over her shoulder. What *had* King Eamon been about, giving his daughter the training of a prince? Granted, Finola *was* the good king's only child and heir, but even so . . .

It just isn't proper, Una decided.

Had these still been the days of Finola's grandfather, Donal-may-his-memory-be-blessed, no young lady, certainly not a princess, would ever have been allowed to go galloping off like a—a headstrong boy.

Och, galloping, indeed. The gatekeepers were casting open the gates at a shout from outside, and here came Finola now, rushing in at the head of a small group of warriors. The girl sat her gray pony as well as any of them, tunic bunched up about her knees, dangling legs protected by boyish leggings and sturdy sandals; the only sign of her royal rank was the golden torc, the short necklace glinting at her throat.

Una shook her head as the riders reined up and dismounted, servants hurrying forward to take their curvetting ponies. Finola was never going to be anything as soft or traditional as pretty, but she certainly was striking, particularly now, with her long hair unraveling from its braids and her blue eyes—Donal's bright blue—so sparkling.

The woman wrinkled up her nose. Striking, too, was the aroma of sweaty pony clinging to the girl, and Una waded into the throng to retrieve her charge.

"Now, is this any way for a princess to look?"

she scolded. "Particularly one who's no longer a child?"

"I suppose not," Finola agreed with a grin. "But wouldn't I look silly riding about checking the condition of my father's fields in a regal gown?"

"Humph, well, never mind. Your royal father has summoned you to him, my girl. Come, you have just time enough to change into something a bit less . . . smelly."

❧

Finola grinned to herself. It was fun riding around the countryside like a boy (even though neither Una nor the girls her own age would ever believe that), but she had to admit it felt good to be dressed more like a true princess again, her blue gown brightly embroidered at neck and hem, her black hair tamed into two neat plaits weighted down by bronze ornaments.

And now to see what Father wants.

A respectful servant held aside the leather curtain covering the doorway to the royal hall, that large chamber with its smooth-packed earthen floor and gleaming wooden walls rimmed with benches for the king's warriors. Finola smiled at the servant and entered—only to stop short, suddenly uneasy. Her father sat alone before the great central hearth, head in hands. He looked so woeful that the girl asked warily: "Father? Are you . . . all right?"

King Eamon glanced up sharply, then very evidently forced a smile on his weary face. "Finola. How went your ride?"

"Well enough." She hesitated, wondering just

how much of the truth he wanted to hear right now, then continued warily, "The spring planting is going nicely, and all should be well if . . ."

"If only the rains come. I know."

Oh yes, if only the rains come, Finola echoed silently, *as they didn't come last year.*

The drought had meant near-disaster for the land, what with the crops failing and her father having to nearly empty the royal treasure just to buy enough grain to keep all his people alive. And if the drought returned this year . . . Finola refused to think of that.

King Eamon cleared his throat nervously. "You don't remember your mother, do you?"

The woman had died when Finola was barely three; all the princess remembered when she tried to think of her mother was someone with warm arms and long, dark hair. "N-not really, you know that. Why are you—"

"I loved her very much. But . . ." The king shook his head. "I shouldn't have let emotion control me. After her death I should have married again, had another heir. I never should have put such a burden on you."

"Irwain is my home! Of course I worry about it! Father, please, what *is* all this? Aren't you happy with me?"

"Oh, love, very happy! No king could wish for a better heir, girl or boy." He took a deep breath. "I received a messenger bird today. The ambassador from Conal of Lerlais will be arriving in a few days."

Finola froze. "Oh, not *that* again! Doesn't he ever give up?"

"Finola, love, I know you didn't like King Conal when you first met him. But you were barely out of childhood at the time, hardly old enough to be a good judge of character."

Old enough, the princess thought bitterly, but said nothing. Eamon smiled uncertainly. "Conal of Lerlais may be some years your senior, but he's still young, and I imagine a woman would find him rather handsome. Would marriage with him be such a dreadful thing?"

"Yes, it would!" Finola snapped, more sharply than she'd intended. Seeing her father stare at her, she hastily continued, "We both know the man isn't madly in love with me. He wouldn't even care if I was ugly or—or stupid as a rock! All he wants is Irwain, and our trading route through the forest with it."

King Eamon sighed. "That, alas, *is* the way the game of politics is played. I thought you knew that."

"Yes, of course, but—"

"Finola, I will admit I had once hoped for a different alliance, one with our other neighbor instead."

"King Anlan."

"Of Taliath, yes." Eamon held up a helpless hand. "Unfortunately, the gods had something else in mind. You know Anlan's older son, Ronan, is already married and expecting his own heir."

"And King Anlan's younger son, Niall, died in a hunting accident a few years ago, when he was about my age. Yes. I do know."

The king reached out to touch her cheek with a

gentle hand. "Which, I'm afraid, really does leave us with only the one other choice: Lerlais, with its young, unmarried ruler."

"Unmarried because he—because his first wife died."

"A tragedy that's several years in the past. And, heartless though it sounds, the death of a sickly young woman hardly concerns us now. My dear, ours, I don't have to remind you, is a very small, very unimportant land. If our ancestors hadn't been clever enough to take advantage of that old forest road, I doubt there ever would have *been* an Irwain! And you—"

He stopped short, so clearly embarrassed that Finola finished drily, "And I'm not exactly the sort of princess the average ruler wants for a wife. You know the sort: beautiful, brainless, and submissive."

"Don't talk like that."

"Father, I know mighty princes aren't going to come suing for my hand. I don't care, n-not really." *Liar!* an inner voice whispered. "But . . ." Struggling for words that weren't too honest, she settled for: "Conal's such a cruel man!"

"You don't know that for sure."

Oh, don't I? But she didn't dare tell him the truth. "I—I've heard so many tales about him from traders—"

"Hardly a reliable source of information."

"Yes, but when all the tales agree, surely *some* of them have to be true! One thing they all have in common is that the man never even laughs." Finola shuddered. *Except when he has the chance to hurt someone less powerful than himself*—No, she couldn't say that to her father, either. "Rather than be forced into some stupid, loveless marriage—yes, and have Irwain's freedom bartered away as well—I'd rather stay unwed."

"You don't know what you're saying, child. Your mother and I—"

"Were fortunate. You were able to wed for love as well as politics. But I—I *won't* be some other king's slave. And I won't see our people turned into slaves, either!"

Her father smiled wanly. "When you talk like that, I see my father in you. Donal was just as fiery when it came to defending the realm! None of this would be necessary if only he'd held fast to Gleaming Bright—"

He broke off so sharply Finola blinked. Had he been afraid to say more? "To . . . whom?" she asked.

"To what," the king corrected reluctantly. "Gleaming Bright was a box, a magical creation, or so my father told me. But it's long lost to us, so there's no reason to give it another thought."

"But—magic—what—Father! You can't leave it like this! *What* box? What happened to it? Was it stolen, or—or . . ."

The man hesitated a long while. "Ah well," he murmured. "What harm to it? You're hardly the sort to go off on some ridiculous quest! So, now: it all started with the wizard Cathbad . . ."

❧

". . . and so," King Eamon concluded, "my father put Gleaming Bright carefully away in a casket in his private chambers, meaning to call upon its powers only in times of direst need. The gods be praised, those times never came. Donal never noticed till the day he died that the casket was empty. When I was newly made king, long before you were born, I had a search mounted for the wizard Cathbad, but my men found no sign of him." Eamon shrugged. "He was elderly even when my father met him, and not even wizards live forever. But I remembered Father mentioning Cathbad's rival, the Dark Druid Rhegeth. And sure enough, my own court druids proved it could only have been Rhegeth who'd stolen Gleaming Bright."

"But what good could it possibly do him? I mean, if only one of our own line can use it— Och, nonsense! That was two generations ago. Rhegeth can hardly still be alive, can he?"

"He *is* a wizard," her father reminded her.

"Well, yes, but if he can't use the box—Father, I don't understand! Why didn't you just send warriors after him to get it back?"

"Ah. Well." Shamefacedly, King Eamon admitted, "Up till this past year, I really had no use for Gleaming Bright. And, frankly, letting Rhegeth keep it, particularly since he couldn't pervert its magic to his own use, seemed safer than going up against the gods know what sorcery. Besides," he added wryly, "right now Irwain is simply too poor to afford any army powerful enough to fight a wizard."

"And Cathbad *did* warn Grandfather to keep Gleaming Bright a secret," Finola added thoughtfully.

"Finola, don't give me that dreamy look. Forget about Gleaming Bright. It's gone, and that's the end of it."

Is it? the princess wondered. But all she said in reply was, "I'll be good. I'll meet with you and the ambassador from Lerlais tomorrow. But I will not make any promises to him—or to his king."

"Fair enough." The king reached out a sudden hand to ruffle her hair, just as he'd done when she was a little girl. "Off with you now."

ᣥ

Her ladies were waiting for her, cheerful, chirpy girls her own age. Finola sat with them as she usually did for part of each day (*my time of traditional princess activity*, she thought wryly), toying with her needlework, dimly aware of their excited gossipings.

"A royal ambassador!" little Baibin was saying amid a storm of giggles. "Isn't it thrilling?"

"And coming here with an offer of marriage, too!" Pretty, plump Ranait dropped her sewing to hug herself in delight. "Oooh, imagine a handsome young king suing for your hand! Isn't it *romantic?*"

"Not so romantic," someone muttered darkly. "Not when it's coldhearted Conal of Lerlais."

"I heard that," Finola said in warning, and the ladies all fell as silent as startled birds. "I don't mean to spoil your fun. But you must watch your tongues. I'm afraid I can't let you slander royalty."

Even when said royalty might deserve—Och, no,

she was being as bad as her ladies. Over four years had passed, after all; Conal *might* have changed.

And horses might have developed wings.

The ladies had warily started their chatter again, keeping to nice, safe subjects: jewelry, gowns, handsome courtiers. But Finola hardly heard their silliness. Pretending to be totally engrossed in selecting just the right shade of red silk thread for an embroidered noble's cloak, she found her thoughts returning again and again not to Conal but to Gleaming Bright.

What a marvel it must be! And how wonderful it would be to have it safe here in my father's house.

With its help (and surely, Finola reasoned, it would help its rightful owners), Irwain would never again be threatened by drought or famine—or ambitious kings, handsome or not.

‌ैं

That night, Finola's dreams were troubled.

She seemed to be looking out over Irwain, but an Irwain laid bare by drought. Not a blade of grass showed green through the burned yellow stubble, not a bird sang in the drooping trees. Finola cried out in her sleep at the sight of the people, her people, trudging wearily from fields that crumbled to powder beneath the plow. She saw the children sitting listlessly in the shadows; she heard a baby crying weakly with the pain of hunger.

No, oh no, please, no . . .

And the dream changed.

All at once something gleamed in her arms:

Gleaming Bright. She recognized the beautiful thing

even though she'd never seen it before. Carefully, the princess opened the box, and a shimmering blue-gray curtain poured out—rain! It was raining, and as she watched, lovely, healthy green spread out over the parched lands. The drought was over, and the crops were fine and full. The weariness was gone from her people's faces, and joyous laughter rang in the air. . . .

The echoes of that laughter were still with Finola when she woke.

The girl rubbed her eyes with a shaken hand. What a strange, strange dream! Part of it had been sparked by her father's tale, of course. And yet . . . magic had glimmered about the whole thing, as surely as magic must glimmer about Gleaming Bright itself.

Almost, Finola thought uneasily, as though Gleaming Bright had, somehow, been calling to her.

No, that's ridiculous! No matter what spells Cathbad placed about it, the thing is still a box, nothing more than a box.

Besides, what good was dreaming? Gleaming Bright was in the hands of a Dark Druid, an evil wizard.

And there, no matter what silliness she dreamed, it seemed likely to stay.

Memories

FINOLA, HER POLITEST SMILE fixed on her face, told herself firmly that she *would* behave. But oh, it wasn't going to be easy!

Surely the ambassador from King Conal of Lerlais had been a weasel in a former life. No, not anything as elegant as a weasel. A snake, maybe, or something slimy. It wasn't that he *looked* unpleasant. On the contrary, not a fold of his long, dark cloak or plain white tunic was out of order, not a strand of his graying brown hair was out of place.

But his smile somehow managed to be both perfectly proper and contemptuous at the same time, and his pale blue eyes held a chill mockery as though he were saying silently, *You're only peasants, both you and your petty little kingdom. You should be honored my king even bothers with you.*

". . . and so, Your Most Gracious Majesty," he continued smoothly, voice urbane, "my master, King Conal of Lerlais, having heard of your daughter's charm and wit"—his flick of a glance told Finola how little he thought of that—"once again expresses his desire to take the Princess Finola to wife."

"We are pleased by—" King Eamon began, but before he could get any farther, Finola, to her horror, heard herself blurt out:

"Why?"

"Finola!" her father whispered sharply, and, "Your Majesty!" the ambassador protested.

Stop it! Finola scolded herself. *Don't say anything else!*

But there wasn't any stopping this ridiculous inner self that had suddenly decided now was a good time to be honest. Helplessly, Finola heard herself continue, quite calmly, "I already have refused your king once. Why won't he give up?"

King Eamon glared at his daughter, then gave the ambassador a charming smile. "She is young. You know how foolish young girls can be."

The ambassador's own smile had never wavered. "Of course," he murmured. "Your Majesty—"

"Excuse me." *Oh, be* quiet! Finola begged herself, but the words still refused to stop. "We all know exactly why King Conal wants to marry me. If I'm wrong, if he really is interested not in Irwain but in me, let him tell me so himself. Till then, Father, my lord, I—I bid you good day."

"Finola!" her father snapped, but the girl pretended she didn't hear him, hurrying from the hall in a swirling of cloak and gown.

She made it all the way to her private chambers, dodging puzzled servants, before she had to stop, biting her lip till it hurt, refusing to weep. It shouldn't hurt like this to know she was only a bargaining chip; every princess was raised knowing marrying for love was an almost impossible dream. And yet—oh, it *did* hurt, it did!

But running away couldn't possibly help. All she'd accomplished by racing out of the hall like a spoiled child was angering the ambassador and her father. And of course they had every right to be angry. In the game of politics, Finola knew, you never, ever spoke the truth outright; you always veiled it in careful, courteous words. What had made her so—so stupidly blunt? And why, oh why, had she run off like this?

Finola shuddered, wrapping her arms about herself. All at once the sight of her father and the ambassador pretending she wasn't even there, of the ambassador's barely hidden contempt for herself and her father, had been too much to bear. She hadn't dared stay in that hall a moment longer.

If I had, I think I would have thrown something at the man. So false, so cold. Like his master.

Suddenly she couldn't stand still. Finola paced restlessly back and forth, trying not to remember. But how could she forget the first time she'd met Conal of Lerlais? It was true, she really had been young, barely into her twelfth year, and rather awed by the sight of the tall, elegantly blond

ed determined to treat his daughter like so
g little girl.

My dear," he said gently, "this hysteria isn'
you."

wasn't hysterical. I only—"

Hush. Listen to me. I know you must be
htened of the idea of marriage. After all, you're
l a child."

"Father, I'm sixteen!"

"Ah. Well." He considered that a moment, then
shed on past it, continuing hastily, "It's natural
ou should be afraid; fear of the unknown is quite
natural thing."

"But I'm not—"

"King Conal of Lerlais is young and ambitious,
with warriors enough to make him a valuable ally
for Irwain—as I thought you understood. And as
such an ally, he would be careful to treat you
well."

The way he nearly raped me on his first visit? No,
she wasn't going to say *that* to her father! "Oh,
yes," Finola said drily. "Until I produced an heir
for him. Then he wouldn't need me anymore.
And he certainly wouldn't need you! Father, I—
I—"

"Now you're just being silly," he soothed.
"Conal won't hurt either one of us."

*No? What about his first wife? The one too sickly
to bear him a child? The one who failed him? For all
I know, Conal murdered her!* Gods, she couldn't
say that, either! "Oh, won't he?" Finola exploded.
"There could be a hunting mishap, tainted food, a

young man who had come to Irwain on a diplo-
matic visit. Her father had entertained him quite
literally royally, hunting with him by day, feasting
with him by night.

*But Father never once noticed how Conal was eye-
ing me. He laughed when I told him, and teased me
about my "suitor."*

The suitor who had cornered her in a quiet palace hallway. At first, Conal had been quite charming, complimenting her on her sleek black hair,
her pretty gown. But bit by bit his compliments
had turned sharp, almost dark. Young as she was,
Finola hadn't been quite sure what he meant, only
that his words were making her strangely un-
comfortable.

I should have run.

How could she? The rules of politics had already
been drilled into her; it wasn't wise to be rude to
royalty. Even such royalty as this man who was
whispering his strange, hot words in her ear.
Nearly sick with fright, Finola had tried her best
to imitate her father, politely asking after the
health of Conal's wife.

"Oh, she's such a sickly thing." Conal's voice
had been so cold and casual it sent shivers all
through Finola. "Unable to bear a child or sit beside me at court. I doubt she'll be with us very
long."

And then . . .

Finola paced even more fiercely, trying to shut
out the memory of his cruelly powerful body suddenly crushing her against a wall, his hand forcing

itself roughly into the bodice of her gown. She'd turned her head sharply away before he could kiss her, but she didn't dare scream; even then she knew that to call for help against a king would involve her father in a crisis that might lead to war.

Instead, Finola had bit his ear, so savagely she'd tasted blood. Conal had hissed in pain, flinging her from him. Hand to his bleeding ear, he'd snarled a warning to her: "If you tell your father about this, I swear I'll kill you, I'll kill all your people!"

Of course, she hadn't said a word. She'd taken to her bed, pretending to be ill, and not a soul had suspected the truth. Conal had left without Finola seeing so much as another hair of his handsome head, and the frightened child she'd been had prayed he would never, ever return.

But she was no longer a child. What Conal had tried to force on her had borne little resemblance to the normal happenings between men and women, she knew that; she'd seen enough happy couples to know such matters were meant to be a joy, not something to dread. Surely even those brought together in arranged matches could still find some delight to take in one another. But with Conal—

Finola's legs suddenly seemed to have lost their power. She sank to her bed, imagining the nightmare of life as Conal's wife, not just in his bed but in every aspect of the day, bound to him by law and politics, subject to his moods and whims and cruelties.

Dear gods, no. I can't mar
I—I won't, I swear it!

Oh, easy to vow! But how bleakly, could she prevent it? telling her father the truth of w back then; that was too politic subject, even now. But what else bly do?

Without warning, thoughts of Gleaming Bright swept back into he sighed impatiently. Dreams. Wha dreams? Oh yes, with such magic, n its very creation could not be misused gain, there would be no reason to Conal or drought or any other perils, bu

"My lady." It was Una, looking at he vere disapproval.

Finola started guiltily. "I know." She g feet with resignation. "My father wishes with me."

As they walked, Una began edgily lecturi princess. Finola caught nervous bits of "How you be so foolish," and ". . . such a fine ma and ". . . running off like a silly little girl!" she ignored it all as best she could, continuing in grim silence.

What a wonderful day this was turning out be.

જ

If only her father would shout at her, or scold her, or even threaten her! Instead, King Eamon fall from a balcony—'Accidents' can happen, and I—I don't want one to happen to you!"

"Nonsense. He wouldn't—"

"Please, listen to me! As you say, Conal is still young; as you say, he's ambitious—but he's also completely ruthless! And that makes him dangerous!"

"Nonsense," Eamon repeated calmly, that infuriating, patronizing note back in his voice. "Finola, I've listened to enough of this. Go back to your chambers and think things over."

"But can't you just—"

"No. I cannot. Go to your chambers and think things over. And in the morning, love, I expect you to have made the proper decision."

His suddenly cold expression left no doubt in Finola's mind as to what that decision was supposed to be.

"Yes, Father," she murmured reluctantly.

THREE

Plots

FINOLA SAT ALONE IN her chamber as her
father had ordered, and as he had also ordered,
did her best to think things over. But she knew
he wouldn't have been pleased at the course her
thoughts were taking.

*I have only two choices, and I d-don't like either
one!*

She could agree to marry Conal. But if she did,
she'd be putting herself, her father, and her land
in peril.

Yet Conal was hardly a patient man or a forgiv-
ing one. If Finola refused to marry him, he would
be furious. Furious enough, perhaps, to decide
that, weak as Irwain was right now, he needn't
bother with any flimsy excuse of marriage. Far easier to soothe injured pride with an invasion.

*We could never hold him off, not in the state the
land is in.* Finola shivered. She had never actually

seen warfare, the gods be thanked, but she'd over-heard enough tales from her father's warriors when they hadn't realized she was listening. It was far too easy to imagine Irwain under siege, its people dying slowly of hunger or more swiftly by the sword or spear, or, maybe worse, being carried off as hopeless slaves.

But what can we do without a strong enough army? Cast spells?

If only they could! But the only charms the gentle court druids knew were healing spells. Only truly powerful magic far beyond their skill would save Irwain.

Magic such as Gleaming Bright—No, stop that! We don't have Gleaming Bright!

But without warning her mind was filled once again with that dream of rain, of green and fertile lands . . .

Gleaming Bright, indeed.

The box had belonged to the wizard Cathbad, and everyone knew how mighty Cathbad had been. But what good was that knowledge now? Finola sighed, pacing once again, moving restlessly from this side of the room to the other. What Irwain needed right now was a hero, some larger-than-life hero out of a bard's tale, the sort of fearless fellow who'd ride boldly into the sorcerer's stronghold, conquer the Dark Druid, and carry off Gleaming Bright in triumph.

What nonsense. There weren't any such heroes in the real world. Beside, she thought with a touch of wry humor, if everything her father had told her was true, no one outside of the royal line was allowed to know about Gleaming Bright anyhow!

Father, I love you dearly, but—but why do you have to be so gentle?

King Eamon had been as bold as his father Donal when he'd been young, so Una had told Finola, but he had ruled a peaceful land so long all the boldness had faded. Not that it mattered, Finola reluctantly admitted: even if he was the boldest man who ever lived, a king could hardly up and abandon his throne to go off on a quest that might be the death of him!

That left only one other person who both knew about Gleaming Bright and was free to go hunting it.

The princess stiffened. "Me?"

Oh no, that was ridiculous. She shouldn't even consider it. Finola hastily resumed her restless pacing, trying to force the thought out of her mind, arguing fiercely with herself. She was a princess, not a—a hero! Maybe she could handle a dagger well enough, and she certainly could use a sling as skillfully as any rabbit-hunting boy, but she wasn't a trained warrior, she didn't know how to manage a sword or spear. This was truly ridiculous, and—and—

And, ridiculous though it might be, terrifying though it certainly was, the idea refused to leave. Recovering Gleaming Bright really did seem to be the only alternative, the only choice with even the slightest chance of bringing happiness.

Gleaming Bright, and the curtain of life-giving rain . . .

Finola sank to her bed. For a long, long while, she sat stock still with shock. And somewhere in the quiet hours that passed it came to her that she'd accepted what must be done.

Aie, and done quickly! Oh gods, yes, to wait even until tomorrow would mean facing her father and the ambassador, and agreeing to be King Conal's wife. Betrothed princesses were kept under such close watch she'd never be able to get away. No, if she was going to leave at all, it would have to be tonight.

I—I can't . . .

But even while some of her thoughts were fluttering about in panic, the rest of her mind had already started planning what must be done:

She would take her warmest, most closely woven (and reasonably waterproof) tunic, leggings, and cloak, of course—an outfit plain enough to be the despair of fastidious Una, maybe, but a good, unremarkable gray and brown, perfect for forest wear. A change of clothing wouldn't add too much weight to her pack and was definitely necessary; she could hardly wear the same outfit all the time, not if she didn't want to come down with some unpleasant skin disease! Combine the clothes with her sturdiest, most comfortable boots, and she should be able to hike for days. Ha, yes, and in that outfit, even if she ran into her father's people in the forest, they'd never recognize her as a princess!

Food. What about food? Ah! She'd add to the pack whatever would keep without spoiling, and depend on her skill with a sling to bring down rabbits and other small game. Mm, she'd better add a packet of healing herbs as well, just in case. There should be clear streams enough to provide water.

Yes, yes, provisions were all well and good, but which way should she go to find Gleaming Bright? There was a vast amount of forest beyond Irwain's walls! But her father had hinted that Rhegeth's *dun*, his fortress, lay somewhere to the west. . . . Vague directions. But the season was spring, the time when the first traders came walking the roads. Surely she would run into some of them. Anyone who depended on wide amounts of travel for his livelihood would almost certainly know the location of that fortress, if only as a place to avoid!

So be it. West she would go, and then . . . only the gods knew what would happen then.

ॐ

Finola mused that getting ready for bed that night, all the while pretending nothing at all was wrong, was surely one of the most difficult things she had ever done. Somehow she managed to keep smiling and nodding and say almost nothing at all as her ladies fussed over her. Somehow she managed not to confess everything to Una as the woman brushed her hair for her, crooning peacefully. As Finola snuggled down into bed, pretending she was too sleepy for speech, Una whispered, "Sleep well, my dove. All will be well, you'll see."

The woman blew out the candle and left.

Suddenly very much alone, Finola gasped out before she could stop herself, "Oh, wait!"

"What's that, my dear?"

"Uh . . . n-nothing. Good night, Una."

There wasn't the slightest danger of falling asleep. Wide awake, wide-eyed, Finola felt as though she would never need to sleep again, waiting out the seemingly endless hours. After an eternity had crawled by, she knew it must at last be past the middle of the night. Trying not to make a sound, the girl slipped out of bed, heart racing, fumbling for her clothes in the dark and feeling hopelessly clumsy. Her boot! Where was her other boot? And the clasp for the cloak was never going to close. . . .

But at last Finola was dressed, her pack slung over her back, and she tiptoed down through the meeting hall, ducking into shadow whenever a weary guard trudged by. She glanced warily out into the earthen courtyard. One more guard was walking out there.

"Go on!" Finola urged him softly. "Go away!"

There, now, he was finally moving away . . . the faint flicker of his torch was fading, fading . . . Now!

Finola darted out and into the building housing the royal kitchens. The kitchen help were asleep in here, snoring gently, and she moved with exaggerated care, gathering provisions into her pack.

She was done. There were no excuses for lingering. Taking a deep breath, the princess stepped back out into the night.

Och, she hadn't had a chance to really notice it before, but it was cold out here, cold and dark! Shivering, Finola pulled her cloak tightly about herself, grateful for its warmth, then started forward, wishing she could somehow steal a horse out of the stables.

Impossible. Someone would be sure to see or hear her. Besides, horses needed grain if they were going to travel a distance, and there was a limit to what she could carry! At any rate, Finola told herself, she could probably work her way through the tangle of forest more easily on foot.

Getting out of Irwain was almost alarmingly easy. Both guards at the palisade's double gate had fallen asleep at their posts. For a moment Finola stood over their huddled forms, hearing them snore, and burned with anger. How *dare* they sleep on duty? She would—

She would do nothing. She wasn't foolish enough to awaken them. Instead, praying there wouldn't be any alarming creaks, the princess pulled one heavy wooden gate open just enough to let her squeeze through, then pushed at its stubborn weight till she had closed it again.

She turned. The forest stood before her, a great, silent black mass in the darkness. For one long, terrified moment, staring at that chill, alien vastness, Finola couldn't move at all.

"Irwain, for you," she murmured at last, and started forward into the night.

FOUR

Forest Dwellers

FINOLA CROUCHED IN THE dense underbrush, trying to ignore the root bruising one knee, hardly daring to breathe as she peered warily through the leaves. There, so close to where she hid that she could hear every word of their muttered complaints, were a band of warriors grimly searching the forest.

Searching for her. Oh yes, she recognized every one of the men. Her father had sent them hunting for her, as he'd sent troop after troop in the last three days.

Of course he had sent them, Finola thought; he could only be thinking she'd run away from home like a little girl angry at her parents. If the warriors caught her, she'd be dragged back in disgrace as though she really was only a child.

"Wish the king had let us take the dogs."

Oh, thank you, Odhran! Finola glared at the stocky, flaming-haired man.

She wasn't the only one who disapproved. Fair-haired Donnan, lean as a hunting hound himself, said sharply, "You don't hunt a princess with dogs!"

"That's right," grim old Dubhan snapped, "shout it out so we can be sure Princess Finola hears us!"

"Och, what difference does it make?" Odhran asked impatiently. "We've been searching for her-self for three days now, without hunting down so much as a hair from her pretty, stubborn head. If we haven't found the princess by now, we're never going to find her."

"Bah," Dubhan said shortly. "She may be a princess, but she's still only a girl. And one girl alone can't possibly escape an entire troop of trained warriors."

"She's done it so far, hasn't she?"

Donnan sighed. "Serves us right for teaching her woodcraft so very thoroughly."

It does, indeed, Finola thought.

But if she stayed here any longer, the men couldn't possibly avoid discovering her. Moving bit by careful bit, the princess backed away on hands and knees, testing each spot before she put her weight on it, biting her lip so she wouldn't make a sound if she landed on a root or a sharp bit of rock. When, after what seemed an eternity, she was finally sure the warriors couldn't see or hear her, Finola got to her feet and hurried off, struggling through the tangle of forest, tripping over roots, snagging clothes and hair on branches. At last, breathless, she sank to a rock, listening feverishly, sure that for all her care, she'd made enough noise in her flight for an army to follow her.

At first all she heard was tense silence, as though the forest was holding its breath. Then the normal little rustlings and stirrings slowly started up again all around her.

Finola let out a long sigh of relief. If the warriors were still following her, the small birds and animals would have remained quiet, frightened by all those noisy, invading human presences. No, she'd escaped yet again. And with any luck at all, the warriors would give up and go home, just like the troops before them. Now all she had to do was puzzle out where her mad rush had taken her.

She . . . *could* puzzle it out, couldn't she?

As Finola stared at the dense, featureless green world about her, a weight of fear settled slowly and coldly into the pit of her stomach. Dear gods, she hadn't the vaguest idea where she was! She didn't know where Irwain lay. She didn't even know which way she was facing! Thin rays of sunlight, dazzlingly gold against the forest gloom, filtered tantalizingly down through the crown of leaves, but there just weren't enough of them to let her judge direction.

That—that's all right. All I have to do is climb a tree.

But when Finola managed to struggle her way

up a wide-limbed oak, she found herself looking out over an unbroken sea of green.

No, oh no . . .

The cold weight of fear was beginning to make her ill. The princess climbed slowly back down, shaking so much she nearly fell. It wasn't so bad, she told herself sharply, it really wasn't so bad. At least now she knew which way was west, and could keep going west by the forester's trick of sighting in a straight line from tree to tree. . . .

Oh, fine. But what small section of "west" did she need? Unless she could find a road, Finola told herself, she wasn't likely to come across any of the traders who were supposed to give her directions to Rhegeth's *dun.* Yet she hadn't seen the slightest hint of even a trail amid all that greenery, let alone a road wide enough to hold a trader's wagon. The Dark Druid's fortress might indeed lie due west of Irwain—but unless she knew where Irwain was, that wasn't going to help very much. She would have to search through all the endless leagues of forest. Assuming, Finola thought bitterly, she managed to survive that long.

It isn't fair. After Irwain suffered through such a drought last year, the forest shouldn't look so green, so lush—so eternal.

The princess sank back to the rock, struggling to hold back tears of sheer panic. How could she have done such a stupid, stupid thing? She was lost, truly, hopelessly lost.

Days later, still traveling desperately west—since there was nothing else she could do—Finola knew she would have welcomed even someone who would carry her home in disgrace.

Home! What a wonderful word!

But just as she'd so foolishly wished, the warriors seemed to have given up the search. She hadn't seen the slightest sign of them, or anyone else, for . . . for however long it had been. Finola licked suddenly dry lips, realizing she'd lost all track of time.

Not that it really mattered. It was full spring in the forest, no doubt about it, with lush greenery on all sides. And part of her was proud of being able to survive in the woodland so well. She could recognize which plants and berries were safe to eat, could successfully hunt down and prepare small game, and had found pure forest streams from which to drink. Her campfires had been as neat and properly sheltered as she'd been taught to build them, and sleeping on beds of pine boughs no longer left her painfully stiff in the morning. Her muscles had toughened up nicely from all the journeying. There wasn't any real danger from wild beasts, not with so much of their natural prey about, and the weather had stayed cooperatively mild; her cloak had indeed proved waterproof enough to keep her dry during the occasional rain.

I should welcome that rain. It shows the drought is over. At least for now.

Back home, the farmers would be starting the spring planting. The spring planting that she wasn't going to see. As Finola hunted for a good place to camp amid the ever-deepening twilight gloom, she had to fight back a sudden surge of tears. What a silly thing to weep about! There would be other springtimes for her to see at home.

But that thought was no comfort just now. Just now she was so lonely she could have screamed.

Och, what was that? The princess froze in sudden alarm, tears forgotten, sniffing the air. Wood smoke! Gods, all she needed now to finish everything off was a forest fire—no, no, the forest was surely too moist for that. Besides, the flickering light she could just about make out through the forest's gloom was too small and controlled to be wildfire.

A homestead! Dear gods, please, could she actually have stumbled across someone's homestead? The thought of a warm bed, a bath, a roof over her head . . . Overwhelmed, Finola hurried forward—

Then stopped short. Who would be living here in the middle of wilderness? Not her father's men, not so far from Irwain. Not farmers, not in such dense forest. Traders? Again, not in dense forest. Foresters? Or someone less honest, someone she really might not want to meet?

At last, impatient with her own caution but refusing to rush, the princess stalked warily forward. Holding her breath, she parted two branches just enough to let her see . . .

No homestead, nothing but a campfire. Three, no, four men sat by the fire, jesting softly as they polished knives: youngish men, maybe, though they were so hard-faced and dirty it was difficult to tell age, ragged as any wolves. Wolves, indeed. These could only be wolfheads, outlaws.

Wonderful. Just what I didn't *need.*

Their leader was standing somewhat apart from the others, and Finola drew in her breath in astonishment. He was startlingly handsome amid all the roughness, his narrow face as elegant as that of someone out of Faerie, his hair softly golden.

Don't be a fool! Finola snapped at herself. Yes, he was beautiful, yes, bards sang of hero-outlaws living in the forest, doing good deeds, but she wasn't about to believe such nonsense. A man who'd lost every sense of law, no matter how handsome he was, was more dangerous than any true wolf.

A hand suddenly clamped down on her mouth, stifling her startled scream.

You see, idiot? They had a scout posted!

As she struggled frantically to draw her knife, a rough arm caught her about the waist. Finola was dragged forward, kicking and clawing, into the circle of firelight, and dumped without ceremony on the ground.

"Hey, look what I caught."

Heart racing, Finola scrambled up, knife in hand, trying to look as dangerous as a wolf herself. The beautiful blond outlaw shook his head in mocking disapproval, smiling.

"Now, sweetling, don't be so fierce." His voice was a purr. "We're not going to hurt you."

His eyes were blue, so very blue. Finola stared into them, fascinated, hearing his voice soothing her, soft as precious velvet. . . .

Someone chuckled, the sound so ugly the princess was jarred back to reality. The other outlaws were all staring at her like so many starving wolves, and Finola fought back a shudder, all too well aware of the harm that could be worked against a woman alone.

The blond outlaw frowned, angry, Finola thought, that his pretty spell had been broken, but he continued suavely, "And what's a pretty creature like you doing all by her lonesome?"

His glance swept over her, making Finola suddenly, ridiculously, aware of how worn and travel-stained she must look. Ignoring the impulse to straighten her tangled braids, she glared up at him. Voice rusty from disuse, she snarled, "That's none of your business!"

The men laughed again, nudging each other, but their leader studied her thoughtfully. "Oh, I think it is," he purred, blue eyes flickering. "I think it's very much our business. In fact, I think we're all going to have a jolly night together." He took a smooth step forward, smiling. "Now, put down that knife, sweetling, and join the fun."

"No." Finola struggled to keep her voice from trembling. "Get back, wolfhead, or I swear I'll cut your pretty face for you."

The man threw back his head in a bark of

laughter, then lunged at her as swiftly as a weasel, catching her about the waist before Finola could react, crushing her against him.

Conal! she thought wildly. *He's just like King Conal!*

The outlaw's hand closed about her knife arm, so tightly that Finola gasped. In another moment she'd have to drop the knife—Curse it, no! She had escaped Conal; she'd escape this man, too!

Fiercely, Finola twisted about and bit the outlaw's hand so hard he yelled, losing his grip on her wrist. The princess lunged up blindly with the knife, feeling it strike flesh, hearing him cry out a second time. He pushed her away, doubling over, hands over her face, swearing in a choked voice. Finola stared in horror at the blood dripping from between his fingers. Oh dear gods, she really *had* cut him!

The other outlaws were locked in shock. In that instant before they could recover, Finola turned and ran.

FIVE

Wolf and Stag

FINOLA RACED THROUGH THE night-black forest with frantic speed, by wild luck dodging branches in the darkness and avoiding roots and rocks. All too soon, the outlaws came storming after her, burning branches clutched in their fists. But the very light that let them see where they were going let Finola see and avoid them.

But I c-can't keep running forever . . . I've got to—got to rest.

At last, breathless, the girl went to earth in a little cave under a mat of tree roots, curling up into as small a bundle as she could manage, struggling not to gasp out loud, trying to be nothing more than one small part of the night. She heard the men crashing all about her for a time, muttering angrily as they searched.

Don't let them find me, please, please don't let them find me!

"It's no good," someone muttered. "She's gone."

"No!" That was their leader, one hand still to his bleeding face. His voice trembling with pain and fury, he snarled, "She won't get away with this. I'll find the little witch no matter how long it takes!"

Finola bit back a frightened whimper. *Don't be stupid!* she snapped at herself. *You've heard enough angry courtiers to know when a man's making empty threats. If he could catch you, he already would have!*

At last, peeking cautiously out of her cramped little cave, she saw the outlaw leader leave. Finola waited for what seemed a lifetime after that, but to her immense relief, the small forest noises finally started up again, telling her that he and his men really were gone.

I fought him, she thought in disbelief. *I fought a man and—and marked him. I won, and I—I—Oh dear gods.*

A sudden surge of memory shook her: *She was a child once more, lying huddled in bed, stunned by Conal's attack, refusing to tell anyone, even worried Una, what had happened.* This attack had seemed so terribly the same, the same horrid strength used against her, the same horrid sense of being . . . unclean. Of being helpless—

No! If there'd been the same attack, there had also been the same defense. She had escaped then; she had escaped now. One thing she was not, Finola told herself sternly, was helpless!

But the fact didn't seem very comforting at the moment. Miserable, tired, frightened, the princess didn't want to be the triumphant warrior just now.

I only want to be safe at home!

Her mind conjured an image of herself in her chambers, surrounded by her ladies, all of them warm and dry and comfortable, and Finola gasped in anguish as a wave of homesickness washed over her. Oh, to be back there, listening to their silly, friendly, happy chatter! And her father—her father must be wondering if she was dead. Dear gods, maybe he'd already held a funeral feast for her!

I'm alive, Father, I'm alive!

Nonsense. He couldn't possibly hear her. She was alone, all alone, with no one to know what became of her. If she hadn't managed to escape, right now those outlaws would be—would be—

I escaped. It's all right. I did escape. And self-pity is stupid. Worse than stupid. Dangerous.

But she kept seeing over and over again the outlaw she'd wounded, hands over his face, and the blood. . . . He'd been so beautiful, so very beautiful. Finola couldn't seem to stop shivering, even after she wrapped her cloak tightly about her.

Dear gods, I want to go home, I just want to go home.

But she was too weary to cling to misery, too weary even to hold to fear. And at last, still huddled in her little shelter, Finola drifted into broken sleep.

A sudden wild rustling in the underbrush woke the princess with a gasp, her heart racing with alarm. Who—what—what was out there? No normal forest creature made so much noise, but the wild rustling didn't sound like anything the outlaws might make. It didn't sound like anything *any* human would make! What manner of . . . monster . . . ?

N-nonsense. There are no such things as monsters.

Weren't there? All of old Una's stories—stories that had seemed so deliciously scary when she'd been a child settled cozily in her bed—came rushing back to her. Biting her lip, Finola lay tightly curled in her little cave like a wild thing hiding from the predators.

No. This was ridiculous. Ignoring a danger didn't make it disappear. Listening to the fierce, frantic rustling, the girl knew she couldn't just go on huddling here. It might be some trick of the outlaws, it might be something far more terrible, but she *had* to know what was out there!

Carefully, almost too stiff to move, Finola struggled to her feet, trying to shake some life back into her cramped body. The moon hadn't quite set, and enough cold silver light filtered down to the forest floor to let the princess stalk forward—trying not to think about outlaws stalking her in turn—and peer carefully through a screen of leaves.

She gasped. This was a stag—but a stag large as a horse, his hide gleaming the most amazing silvery white!

Animals sometimes are born pure white, she reminded herself. *There's nothing magical about it.*

Peering through the early-morning gloom, Finola realized that the stag had somehow managed to trap his majestic, branching antlers in a net of branches and couldn't get loose for all his struggles. Poor beast! If she left him here like this, he would surely starve. If wolves or hungry outlaws didn't find him first.

But a trapped, frightened animal could be dangerous, and this was a very large stag. Finola approached very carefully, crooning softly to him, "I'm not going to hurt you, you lovely thing. Just stay still, and I'll get you out of this. Just stay still."

One silvery ear flicked in her direction, one large, dark, white-rimmed eye rolled back to watch her. As Finola drew her knife, she saw every muscle tense, but the stag remained perfectly still as she worked his antlers free from the branches, tine by tine.

"There! You're free!"

The stag was gone in one mighty bound. Finola barely stifled a sob of loneliness, because after his dazzling white vitality, the forest seemed all at once very dark and empty. But just as suddenly he was back, staring at her. His mouth opened. And a voice distorted but still quite understandable said: "Thank you."

SIX

Companions
on the Road

FINOLA STUMBLED BACK IN sheer terror, staring at the stag. "You—you *spoke!*" Oh gods, no, this was impossible, animals couldn't talk! She—she must be going mad from the stress of that narrow escape or maybe from sheer loneliness!

"I . . . did." The words came haltingly from a mouth not shaped properly for them. "I . . . am in . . . your debt."

"B-but this is insane!" Finola gasped out. "You're a *stag!* Stags can't speak! How—how can you be speaking?"

The sound the stag made could almost have been a chuckle. "I don't know." His words seemed to be coming more easily with practice. "My memory is . . . is . . . hazy. But I think I could . . . imitate the words of hunters and woodsmen . . .

right from . . . from fawnhood." He paused, considering. "I think it must have frightened my mother."

"I imagine it did!" Finola heard herself giggle nervously and told herself sharply, *Stop that!* "I'm finding it difficult enough to believe this, and I'm human!" She grabbed frantically at the only explanation that came to mind. "I—I guess some wizard must have been working a spell nearby while your mother was carrying you. His magic must have brushed you in the womb."

"Perhaps." The stag didn't seem very concerned about it; animals, after all, Finola reminded herself, simply accepted things as they were. "You are human . . . human," the stag continued.

"Finola. My name is Finola."

"Finola," the stag repeated carefully, then stopped. "A name? That is . . . what?"

"What I call myself. What people call me."

The stag paused again, plainly confused. "I . . . don't think I *have* a name," he said at last.

"No, I—I wouldn't suppose you would."

"Ah well," the stag decided, "they are human things, these names, not for such as me. But I will not run from them. Finola, it was your human hands that saved me." His dark eyes were somber. "Had you not freed me, the wolves would almost certainly have caught me."

"You—you're quite welcome." Finola drew back in sudden new caution. "Why are you talking like that? You're beginning to sound more like a courtier than a woodsman."

The dark eyes blinked in confusion. "I don't understand."

"Your speech! Woodsmen don't talk so grandly."

The stag stirred uneasily. "It is the way I always speak. When I do speak. Why does that bother you?"

Finola sighed. Who could tell what weird paths magic might take? If the excess power of a spell was going to give a beast human speech at all— yes, and what seemed to be a good approximation of human thought, too—it might as well give him noble speech as well! "Never mind. It's not important."

The stag snorted, a very animal sound, and stamped one hoof impatiently. "As I first said, I am in your debt." He paused. "That *is* what humans would say, isn't it?"

"Uh . . . yes."

"Well, then! What may I offer you in return?"

Finola hesitated, trying to find a tactful way to say that there really wasn't anything an animal could do for her.

Or was there? She shivered as a surge of hope and fear all tangled together rushed through her. The stag belonged to this forest; surely he knew everything within it. Everything—and everyone. "Have you," the princess began carefully, "ever heard of the Dark Druid, Rhegeth?"

The stag started back, staring at her in horror, silvery hide shuddering. "Yes, oh yes. All who are of the forest know of him. Why do you ask?"

She didn't dare mention Gleaming Bright, not

even to an animal. "I . . . uh . . . need to find his *dun*, his fortress. Do you know where it lies?"

"No! Yes! I mean, why would you ever want to go there?"

"I must."

"You don't understand! Rhegeth is a cruel, cruel man, a—a monster! His powers are as evil as his heart, and his mind is full of strangeness. He has done terrible things to beasts, yes, and humans, too! Whenever he acts, the forest reeks of fear and pain!"

Oh, dear gods . . . "I—I'm sure it does."

The stag sniffed deeply. "You don't smell of evil; you can't be his friend."

"I'm not."

"Then you *can't* mean to just walk into his grasp! Surely you have a home? Yes, yes, of course you do. Humans have such things. Don't go seeking your doom, Finola. Go home."

"I can't," she said unhappily. "Not yet. Stag, I don't know how much you can understand of this, but . . . well, Rhegeth stole something from my grandfather, something so important to my people that I—just can't go home without it."

The stag stared at her for a long time, his large brown eyes very serious. At last he shuddered and looked away, proud head drooping. "No," he murmured. "I don't really understand. But a stag will sacrifice himself for his does, and a doe for her fawn. Is this human matter of yours something like that?"

"Yes."

"Then . . ." he continued reluctantly, "come with me, Finola. I will take you to that dark place. And perhaps we may still manage to live happily after that. Or," he added dourly, "at least live."

❧

At first, Finola couldn't think of a thing to say to her guide. What could one possibly discuss with a stag? Even a moon-white, intelligent, talking stag? She wasn't about to babble something foolish such as, "Do you like being a stag?" or "How do leaves taste?"

Surely the stag wasn't any more at ease with her than she was with him. After all, even though he'd been brushed by magic, he was still a wild animal. Every instinct must be screaming at him to run away from this stranger, this *human*. Humans killed stags! Finola swallowed drily, wondering if her guide could somehow tell she'd eaten venison.

If he did, he hid his distaste very well. When the forest permitted, the stag walked quietly by her side. When the undergrowth grew too dense, he led the way along narrow, winding paths that must surely be deer trails. Finola followed, feeling hopelessly clumsy and noisy in his silent, graceful wake, fighting the thought that he was either going to deliberately get her lost—or more lost than she already was—or, since he was an animal, simply forget all about her. At least she felt a good deal safer as far as the outlaws were concerned having him about: those great antlers were like a gleaming mass of swords.

The day slowly worked itself about towards twilight. "You cannot see in the dark, can you?" the stag asked suddenly.

"Uh, no."

"Well then, you must spend the night here. I will return later."

"Oh, but don't—"

But he had already vanished into the forest. After a nervous time, Finola realized he must be giving her a chance to eat the rations of dried meat she had with her without having to feel guilty about it.

I suppose he will return, just as he said. At least, she added to herself, glancing uneasily about at the dark mass of forest, *I hope he does.*

He did. That night, Finola woke to find the stag standing watch like some gleaming guardian.

ॐ

By midday of the second day, the awkward near-silence between girl and stag had grown until Finola couldn't stand it any longer. This was ridiculous! She had to say *something!*

"Do you—" the princess began, just as the stag started. "Are you—"

They both broke off, then started to laugh, she in human fashion, he with odd little chuffles.

The stag dipped his head politely. "You first."

Finola felt herself redden. Feeling foolish, she murmured, "I was only going to ask what it was like living in the forest."

The stag repeated his little chuffle. "What would you have me say? There are times of terror, of winter cold and bitter, bitter hunger, of wolfsong thin on the edges of sound."

Finola stared at him in wonder. "You sound like a poet."

"Poet?" the stag echoed carefully, then shook his antlered head. "The word doesn't mean anything to me."

"No. I guess it wouldn't."

"Ah, but you should not have the wrong thoughts about the forest! There are also times of great beauty here. Have you ever watched the moonlight make each leaf glint and glitter? Or seen the sunrise come stealing into the forest, bit by golden bit? Or watched each new bud swell into springtime life?" He let out a gusty sigh. "It is often lovely here, and I could be truly happy here, if . . ."

Finola prodded warily, "If!"

The stag shuddered. "If I wasn't the only one of my kind."

"I'm sorry. I didn't mean to—"

"It is not your fault!" He snagged a flower in his antlers and lowered his head to her. "Here."

With an embarrassed little giggle, she took it, and the stag laughed. "Maybe you are not my kind. Maybe none are. But how could I possibly be lonely with such a friend? Come, Finola-friend, we still have a long way to go."

❧

". . . and so the fox dropped the whole honeycomb and dove headfirst into the lake!"

Finola burst into laughter. "I can guess he never tried raiding bees again!"

The stag gave his odd, throaty little chuckle. "I suppose not," he agreed, eyes bright with amusement.

What an entertaining companion he was turning out to be! Finola thought in amazement. Of course animals had a sense of humor; anyone with a pet dog or cat knew that. But the stag, the princess realized, had a lovely, sharp wit that—well, it was almost human. Maybe he couldn't really understand the stories she told him in exchange for his forest tales—how could he, after all, know anything at all about the world of kings and politics?—but he certainly had a fine taste for the ridiculous.

"Then there was the squirrel I saw—"

The stag broke sharply off, head raised, scenting the wind. "Humans," he said shortly. "Hunters. Following us."

The outlaws? Och, it didn't matter whether these were outlaws or ordinary hunters, not with the stag's white coat like a shining beacon! "You have to hide!"

But the stag was still intently sniffing the air. All at once he snorted angrily. "The wind changed. I can't smell them anymore. A storm's coming."

"Oh, wonderful!"

"Come, this way. Shelter."

A great tree had fallen aslant against a boulder; enough time had passed for a whole new thicket of young growth to have sprung up on and about it. The stag scrambled nimbly up a pile of broken rock, nosing his way through the vegetation. He worked his way into the little triangle of space formed by tree and rock, settling inside, folding his long legs neatly. Finola squirmed in beside him, smelling his warm, wild animal scent all around her, feeling his warmth, her heart racing. The forest was rapidly darkening as the storm clouds rushed in overhead, but if she peered through the tangle of leaves, she could catch glimpses of a ragged man, bent nearly double as he followed their track.

He won't be able to track us over rock, and—Dear gods, those are *the outlaws!*

There was no mistaking their leader, his once-handsome face half-hidden by a grubby bandage. His eyes glinted feverishly in the dim light, bright, bright blue. "She's here somewhere." His voice drifted up to her. "Find her!"

"Oh stag," Finola whispered, "he isn't hunting you, he's hunting me!"

SEVEN

The Black Lands

"HE HUNTS YOU!" THE stag whispered in astonishment. "Why?"

How could Finola possibly explain how humans acted? "He . . . caught me and tried to hurt me. I hurt him instead and escaped. I n-never thought he would track me like this."

"And how are we to be rid of him?"

"I don't know." A sudden dazzling flash of lightning made her start. As thunder shook the ground, Finola tensed, staring thoughtfully up. "Wait, now. . . . Yes, I think I do know a way at that. Listen and tell me what you think of this. . . ."

She whispered her plan in the stag's ear and heard him chuffle with amusement. "Clever, oh clever! Yes," he agreed, "I know just the place. Come."

He led her on a wild scramble up the hillside until they reached an exposed overhang of rock looking out over the forest below. It was not, Finola thought, working her careful way out onto the rock, the place she really wanted to be during a thunderstorm, but if this plan worked . . .

"Ho, you who trespass in the forest!"

My, how nicely her voice rang out! *So* impressive. Ah, and look at the outlaws start! She saw their leader point angrily up at her, and hastily continued before he could say anything, "You have walked where none should walk. No one human!"

With that, the stag stepped lightly out onto the rock with her. As nicely as though they'd timed it, a white-hot flash of lightning cut the sky at that very instant, turning the stag's coat to blazing silver. The outlaws' shocked cries drifted up to her, and Finola shouted with all her might, "You are doomed! You are all doomed!"

In the next moment a stupendous clap of thunder shook the earth. Ha, wonderful, now the outlaws were definitely nervous! Even though their leader was arguing with them, waving his hands about angrily, they really did think she was something Other, she and the stag both. One more good shout should do it. "Run, you fools! Run before I take your lives, your hearts, your very souls!"

Lightning flared with her words. And that was just too much for the outlaws. They turned as one man and ran, trailed by their furious leader, and Finola hurried them along by sending eerie peals of laughter after them.

The laughter faded to normal giggles. The stag nuzzled her cheek. "Nicely done," he murmured. "Now let's get back into shelter before the rain starts."

They huddled together in the tiny cave of trunk and rock, warm and dry, listening to the rain pour down all about them.

"Did you see them run?" Finola said suddenly. "Did you? They aren't going to be bothering us again!"

"True. But they were an easy foe."

"Easy!"

"Compared to the Dark Druid," the stag said quietly, "they were no more than shadows. Think of that, Finola. Think."

Finola bit her lip. "I have. Stag, no matter what you say, I'm still going on."

He sighed. "You are like a fawn who thinks himself a mighty stag because he's chased away a rabbit. But . . . so be it. We will go on."

❧

Finola was asleep, drifting deeper and deeper into dreaming. She was vaguely aware this was only a dream, and yet at the same time it seemed far, far too real. . . .

Her father sat alone in his hall, head down, hand covering his face, and Finola knew with a dreamer's certainty that he sat mourning her.

"Father, don't! It's all right, I'm alive."

But she couldn't seem to make him hear her, no matter how hard she tried.

What was this? The ambassador from Conal of Ler-

lais had somehow appeared in the hall, his face contorted with fury. "You have betrayed my king!" he shouted at her father. "You have cast a grave insult at him! You have deliberately hidden your daughter so there can be no wedding!"

"No!" Finola shouted. "That's not true!"

Neither her father nor the ambassador seemed to hear her. "But you shall not be allowed to make a mockery of us!" the ambassador continued fiercely. "If my king cannot have your land through peaceful alliance, then he shall take it by force! You shall pay for your cunning, yes, you and all your people! You shall pay!"

All at once the hall was full of armored men, rushing forward with swords drawn. Courtiers came running in to stop them, only to be cut down. The air rang out with their cries of despair, and at last no one was left alive save for her father, standing trapped by a mound of bodies—

"No, oh no," Finola shrieked, "I didn't mean for this to happen. I only wanted Irwain to be safe. Oh Father, I—I'm sorry, I . . . Please, listen to me!"

But he was turning his face from her. Finola cried out in pain . . .

. . . and woke with her face wet. Dear gods, what a dream. Och, and let it be only a dream! She'd never stopped to think what the ambassador's reaction might be to her disappearance; for all she knew, he really *had* exploded with anger or gone charging back to Conal.

Why didn't I stop and think of that? Why did I just go running off?

Because, deep within her, Finola realized, she had never expected her journey to take so long. Because she'd thought to find Gleaming Bright right away and carry it off with no difficulties at all—Gods, why had she been so foolish?

Shaken by her despair, Finola curled into a tight ball, aching for her father, for everyone in Irwain.

"Oh don't," the stag said helplessly. His soft nose nuzzled her cheek, his tongue licked away a tear. "Don't grieve."

Finola sniffed, uncurling, wiping her eyes dry with a hand. "How could you know how I felt? Deer don't weep."

"But they do grieve. They may not leak this salty water from their eyes, but I do know the feel of unhappiness."

"I—I'm sorry. Of course you do." Finola gave a shaky sigh. "I was dreaming. About h-home . . ."

She was *not* going to start weeping again!

The stag hesitated, then folded his legs to lie beside her, the warmth of him wonderfully inviting. Finola tentatively reached out a hand to touch his soft, smooth coat, then leaned against him, hearing his heart beat, smelling the sharp, though not unpleasant, scent of him. He wasn't quite happy about being touched; she could feel the wild animal tension tightening his muscles, but she couldn't bear to let go, not quite yet.

At last, with a sigh, the stag turned his head and rested his chin lightly on her head.

"Friend," he murmured.

"Friend," Finola agreed.

How long had they been traveling? A week? A month? Finola frowned to realize that once again she'd lost all track of time. But time really didn't seem to matter anymore. There was only the forest, as though there had always been only the forest, and the stag ever by her side as the season ripened through springtime into early summer.

My father wouldn't recognize me, Finola thought ruefully, trying to ignore the sudden sharp little pang of homesickness that realization brought. *I look like a wild thing myself, all rags and roughness.*

She'd done her best to keep herself and her clothing clean, but streams and rain just didn't take the place of a nice hot bath. And soap. Finola knew she had never appreciated the art of soapmaking before she'd had to make do with the occasional cleansing herb she'd found.

Ah well, at least she wasn't alone. Finola admitted to herself that she was never going to quite forget this was an animal walking at her side, no matter how magical he might be. But as the days passed, it was becoming less and less strange to be carrying on a conversation with, or jesting with, or just enjoying the company of a stag. Whatever else he might be, he was as true a friend as any she'd ever had.

"Stag," Finola began hesitantly, rather hoping he felt the same way about her. But right then they reached the top of a small hill just tall enough to give them an overview of the land ahead, and the princess forgot what she'd been about to say, stopping so sharply she nearly fell. "What in the name of all that's holy is *that?*"

Ahead of them, the forest changed, as suddenly as though someone had drawn a line. Here, all was normal, healthy, sweet-scented greenery. There, nothing grew but gnarled, ugly, twisted trees, trees that were dull black of trunk and leaf and long, reaching thorns.

"That dark and deathly place," the stag said softly, "marks the edge of Rhegeth's realm. Finola, please, there is still time to turn back."

Staring at the horror, she shivered, aching to give up, to run all the way back to human lands and warm, familiar safety. But her mind offered her an image of Irwain under drought, as it had been last year. Just as now, the rains had allowed spring planting, but then they'd fled. All summer the sun had shone without mercy, blighting the seedling crops. And oh, even if the drought did not return, nothing had been settled about Conal and the chance of his invasion.

"I—I can't," Finola whispered in despair. "I must go on."

But a wry corner of her mind added sharply, *Gleaming Bright, you'd better be worth all this, or I swear I'll toss you into the deepest, darkest pit I can find!*

"I must go on," Finola repeated slowly. "But there's no reason for you to put yourself in danger. I can surely find my way from here."

"No." The stag straightened defiantly. "I promised to show you the way to the Dark Druid's fortress, and so I shall."

"I . . . thank you."

Together, they stepped across the invisible boundary and entered the dark forest.

EIGHT

An Old Friend Returns

FINOLA GLANCED UNEASILY ABOUT, as she'd been doing ever since she and the stag had crossed over from live forest into . . . this place, however many hours ago it had been. On all sides, twisted trees seemed to be reaching up in supplication, writhing in silent, endless pain. There was no underbrush at all, save for a few low tangles of dry, leafless branches, all of which seemed to bear thorns like small knives, and not the slightest sign of life, not a blade of grass, not the faintest chirp of a bird.

Of course not, Finola thought. *What sensible bird would perch in such a place? And what could grow in all this darkness?*

Although she knew that somewhere far overhead the sun must be shining, down here all was black, from the charred bark of the trees to the soft powder of long-dead leaves whispering softly beneath feet and hoofs. Anyone could be stalking them, or . . . anything.

I won't keep looking behind me, Finola determined, then found herself glancing back over her shoulder anyhow. Angry at herself for this weakness, she turned resolutely forward and found the stag watching her. "I don't like this forest," the princess murmured by way of excuse. "I don't like anything about it."

Now isn't that a stupid thing to say! she scolded herself. *How could anyone like such a grim place? Anyone normal, that is.*

Who knew? Maybe Rhegeth enjoyed all this lifeless darkness! Maybe he found it . . . restful.

A shudder shook the stag's gleaming white coat. "This is *his* work," he said softly, and Finola didn't have any question about whom he meant. "I doubt he did this deliberately, but it was surely *his* sorcery that drained the life from this place." The stag's nostrils were pinched with distaste. "Phaugh, yes. I can smell the reek of that sorcery all around us."

"How far do you think this . . . forest extends?"

The stag hesitated thoughtfully, as though testing some wild creature senses beyond the mere physical. "I'm not sure," he said at last. "Not *too* far, I think."

"It had better not be too far! Otherwise, I don't know what we're going to do for food or drink.

I'm almost out of supplies, and you surely can't find anything worth eating here."

The stag shivered again. "There's *some* healthy greenery surviving amid all the deadness. And there must be something for you, as well. *He* has to eat, doesn't *he?*"

"I wonder." *Don't be ridiculous,* Finola snapped at herself, *whatever else Rhegeth may be, he's still flesh and blood!* "Of course he does. And if he—What is it?"

The stag inhaled sharply, snorted, then scented the air again. "I'm not sure," he said impatiently. "The reek of this place tends to drown out other odors." He waited tensely for a time, head up, fiercely alert, Finola every bit as tense, then lowered his head with a sigh. "Nothing, now. The daylight is quickly running out; I fear we must spend a night here."

Finola shuddered. She'd never be able to sleep in this dark place, never.

But, much to her amazement, once she'd settled down as best she could, sheer weariness of mind and body eventually won out over nerves. And sleep, she did.

≀▲

Finola woke with a shock. What? Who? A hand was clamped roughly over her mouth, a rank human body was crushing her against the ground! Struggling for breath, she managed to squirm one arm out from under this sudden terrifying weight, clawing up. Her hand encountered cloth, a bandage—the outlaw leader!

In the next moment, the stag came rushing forward, bellowing, gleaming antlers lowered. The crushing weight was suddenly gone from her as the outlaw scrambled desperately back.

"Demon," he gasped, "demon," then crumpled bonelessly and lay still. The stag stood over him uncertainly, head down, antlers still lowered in menace.

"No, wait." Finola moved warily to the man's side, bending to cautiously touch his brow. "I don't think he knows what he's doing. He's blazing with fever." No wonder, with that grimy bandage covering his wound.

The wound she'd caused. Finola fumbled with her flint and steel until she'd struck a light. No problem finding dry wood here; the problem, instead, would be in keeping the whole dead forest from catching flame. With one hand, gritting her teeth against the too slippery feel of powdered leaves, the princess cleared a bare spot and stuck a burning branch into it to serve as a torch.

"What are you doing?" the stag asked sharply. "He hunted you. Leave him."

Staring down at the unconscious man, Finola told herself the stag was right. It was ridiculous to feel responsible for the outlaw's wound, when all she'd been trying to do was defend herself. But to leave someone, even an outlaw, to die of fever and exposure, particularly *here* . . . No.

Every young woman, royal or not, learned at least the rudiments of healing, and the princess cut away the bandage with the care she'd been taught, bracing herself. Ah. The wound wasn't so bad, a shallow, straight slash across one cheek—or it wouldn't have been so bad, if the man had thought to care for it properly. Finola hesitated, studying the angry inflammation by the flickering firelight, then used some of her precious water to wash the slash as clean as she could.

There should be some herbs left in my pack . . . yes.

Sprinkling the wound with dried comfrey, Finola bandaged it with a clean strip of cloth torn from her tunic, then sat back on her heels.

"That's the best I can do for him. What happens now is up to him."

"Huh," the stag muttered. "If we're lucky, he'll run off in the night. Or die."

"Stag!"

He snorted. "I'll keep watch. See if you can go back to sleep, Finola. You will need your strength."

❧

"Good morning."

Finola sat up in alarm, hastily wiping her eyes clear of sleep. The outlaw was sitting with his back to a tree, looking gaunt but clear of eye in the early-morning light and, despite the bandage, still so handsome her heart seemed to miss a beat or two. He was holding her water pouch, and she snatched it back with a sudden gasp of alarm, wincing to feel how nearly empty it was.

"This is the only water we have!"

"You wouldn't begrudge a poor, sick man a sip,

would you?" He started to smile, then winced, hand going to the bandage. "Particularly no one whose life you've saved."

"I didn't save your life," Finola snapped. "Your fever must have been just about to break anyhow; the little I did wouldn't have made such a miraculous change."

"Tended me, then. Ministered to my wound."

For a heartbeat's time, something odd hinted in his eyes, something almost chill, and Finola added sharply, "I didn't intend to do that, either. I just didn't want to leave anyone lost . . . here."

"Ah yes. Here." The outlaw glanced about, and a flicker of uneasiness crossed his face. "This is a strange place in which to find such a lovely young woman."

"Stop that."

"But you *are* lovely, even underneath all that grime."

"Don't be ridiculous." Finola could feel her face reddening and scrambled to her feet, pretending to be very interested in brushing herself off. She hesitated, then bent to touch his brow. His hand shot up to close about her wrist, and for a moment Finola froze, staring down at his so very blue eyes. But all at once he laughed, shattering the moment, and she snatched her arm away. "You're no longer feverish. The healthy forest is back that way. Go."

"Ah, but how can you be sure I'm not fevered? You haven't done more than merely brush my poor, weary brow."

Grinning, he swiped at the hem of her cloak. Finola angrily tugged it free. "Don't do that."

Where was the stag? Why wasn't he helping her against—against—

"Do what?" the outlaw asked innocently. "I am in your debt, sweetling."

His eyes were very blue, very bright. . . . Finola turned sharply away, reminding herself that this wasn't some safe, pretty courtier flirting with safe, pretty words. He was an *outlaw:* an outlaw whose face she'd scarred. "Don't call me that. My name is Finola."

Gods, what had made her tell him that? Her name was none of his business.

"A lovely name. And I . . ." He shrugged. "Call me Fiain."

" 'Lawless,' eh?" Finola snorted. "It suits you."

He bowed from the waist, then got carefully to his feet. As he did, the color faded from his face. "Och. I'm not as well as I thought. What are you doing in this dreadful spot, Finola?"

"It's hardly your business."

"You wound me, sweetling, with your coldness."

"Oh, *will* you stop that? Maybe I'm here to—to work a spell!"

He chuckled, the warmth of it prickling up her spine. "Maybe the others believed you're some fear-some sorceress. I know you're just a girl. A lovely one, perhaps, but still just a girl."

That stung. "Get out of here."

"I hate to admit this, sweetling, but I . . .

don't think I have the strength. Will you come with me?"

"No."

"Ah well, then I'll just have to go along with you."

"No!" But he really wasn't in any condition to travel through the forest alone. Finola hesitated nervously, not sure what to say or do next, then straightened with a little sigh of relief. The stag had returned. He stepped softly out of dark forest to her side, white coat gleaming, and she saw Fiain's eyes widen in astonishment.

"A pretty pet!"

Finola ignored him. "Where were you?" she whispered to the stag. "What am I supposed to do with him?"

The stag merely stared at her, eyes blank as those of any plain, unmagical animal.

"Stop that!" Finola hissed. "Please! I don't know what to do!"

He opened his mouth—then yawned and lowered his head to nibble an itch away from a foreleg. Finola stared at him, furious. What in the name of all the gods was he trying to do?

All right, play your little game! I—I'll make my own decision. "Yes," she said to the outlaw. "You may travel with us. For now."

But she couldn't keep from wondering, seeing the sly glint of his blue eyes, if she'd made a terrible mistake.

NINE

Decisions

FINOLA GLANCED AT FIAIN in annoyance for what seemed like the hundredth time. "Will you *please* stop crowding me!"

"Was I?" His smile was the essence of innocence. "My pardon, sweetling. I'm still not quite steady on my legs."

"Huh."

"It's only been a day, after all." Finola pulled angrily away as his hand brushed hers a little too deliberately for it to have been an accident. He gave her a mock-piteous look. "You can hardly expect me to have regained all my strength so quickly, now, can you?"

"J-just keep your hands to yourself."

Grinning, Fiain held up both hands. "See? Your wish, sweetling, is my—"

"And stop calling me that!"

"Whatever you say, my dear Finola, whatever you say."

But his eyes continued to glitter with such amusement Finola ached to slap him. It had been like this all day, he always walking just a bit too close to her, always seeming to be finding an excuse to touch her, never quite in an offensive way. And every time she tried to complain, Fiain would claim that his weakness put him in need of support, all the while those lovely blue eyes of his most disconcertingly gave away nothing of his true thoughts. What could she do? Call him a liar? It wasn't as though he'd actually done anything wrong, after all.

What does he want of me? She could feel herself starting to blush at that, and added wryly, *Besides that, I mean. He can't have forgiven me so easily for wounding him. Ha, and for wounding his dignity as well! Or can he? It . . . can't be the start of something more, can it? He . . . can't possibly be . . . falling in love with—Och, that's the most ridiculous thing! He's an outlaw, not some dewy-eyed my-all-for-romance courtier! In Fiain's case, if it's anything at all, it's falling in lust. And I am not going to fall with him!*

"Ha, look!" Fiain cried suddenly. "A rabbit!"

The poor, frightened thing must have gotten itself lost in these dead lands. Finola felt a little pang of pity stab through her at the thought, but she didn't let that stop her from quickly fitting a stone to her sling and firing.

"Oh, good shot!" Fiain crowed, racing to the kill. He held the rabbit up with a rueful frown. "Skinny thing. It isn't going to go very far between the two of us, now, is it?"

Finola took the rabbit from his hands and set about efficiently gutting it, long past the point of squeamishness, silently thanking her father's warriors as she did, as she had ever since she'd begun this journey, for having taught her how to prepare game for carrying. "It will do, at least for now. We were almost out of provisions."

Fiain gave her a sharp little grin. "I always do enjoy a bit of fresh meat!"

Finola shot him a wary glance. Trust the man to give even the most innocent of statements a double meaning! "Indeed," she said flatly as they traveled on.

At least she didn't have to worry about feeding the stag, too. He seemed to be managing well enough, nosing out enough little patches of healthy vegetation, startlingly green against the darkness, to keep him fed.

But Finola thought unhappily that ever since Fiain had joined them, the stag had been avoiding her, moving silently through the forest at some distance from her, giving the princess only quick, ghostly glimpses of his white coat.

What's wrong with him? I know he doesn't like Fiain, but surely he knows Fiain isn't going to hurt him. Finola swallowed convulsively, blinking fiercely. *We were having such fun together. I thought we were friends, true friends. D-doesn't he realize how much I miss him?*

"Hey now, water!" Fiain said suddenly, and snapped Finola back into the present. "A whole pool of it." But then the man stopped, eyeing it dubiously. "Do you think it's safe?"

Finola crouched down, studying the pool carefully. "I think so," she said after a moment. "It's being fed by a spring. See, over there? That means the water's coming from far below the surface, somewhere down in the clean earth. As long as we drink directly from the spring, I think we should be all right." She got quickly to her feet as the stag appeared suddenly at her side, watching him scenting the water busily. *Say something!* she begged him silently.

But, still without a word, he stepped gracefully forward and began to drink. Finola sighed. "There's our answer," she said.

Watching as the outlaw removed his bandage and began gingerly washing his wound, the princess struggled for something encouraging and safe to say. "It's healing nicely," Finola called out at last.

Fiain ignored her completely. As he caught sight of his reflection for the first time, he stiffened, then traced the line of the slash with a wary forefinger, his face gone very still and cold.

"I . . . uh . . . don't think there'll be much of a scar," Finola added as cheerfully as she could, thinking, *I sound like one of those disgustingly chirpy little birds.* "I . . . didn't really want to hurt you, you know. I was just defending myself."

He glanced her way, and for one heart-stopping moment his eyes were still chill as stone. But in the next instant the coldness was gone, and Fiain was laughing. "Why, sweetling, don't look so worried! It's an honor to wear the mark of so lovely a lady!"

She reddened as he continued to laugh.

༂

As the daylight faded, Fiain sat near the princess, watching her arranging her sadly bedraggled cloak as best she could as a blanket. "Hey now, sweetling, I have a suggestion!" the outlaw said lightly. "Why don't we sleep together tonight?"

"What!"

"I meant only for warmth." He grinned. "Why, sweetling, what did you *think* I meant?"

Finola could feel herself starting to blush all over again. "Stay where you are. I'm warm enough."

"Ah, such a brave thing. So young, so alone. So very pretty." Somehow, Finola wasn't quite sure how, he'd subtly edged forward so that now he was sitting very close to her, hand not quite resting on her knee. "Why are you here, Finola?" he crooned. "What treasure can you possibly be hunting?"

"Is that it?" she asked sharply, pulling away. "You've been following me all this way because you think I'm after *treasure?*"

He frowned. "Then why *are* you traveling

through such a dead place?" Fiain paused, studying her, one brow raised in curiosity. "What's haunting you, sweetling?"

"Nothing to worry you."

"Now, did I say I was worried? But you look so very much in need of comforting. And I am very good at comforting."

His lips met hers before she knew what he meant to do, so gently, so tenderly the tears came to her eyes. "Don't . . ." she began, thinking, *This is stupid, I mustn't—*

But now he was kissing her again, and this time there was nothing gentle about it. Suddenly she was twelve years old again and struggling against Conal, wild with panic—

"Sweetling, sweetling! I'm not going to hurt you. Here, let's try this again."

"I don't want—"

But his lips were already on hers, gentle again, his arms closing about her with soft, implacable strength, and Finola, wild with confusion, didn't know if she wanted to push him away or pull him closer—

A roar of fury split the air. With a startled shout, Fiain pushed her from him, scrabbling frantically backwards on hands and rump as the stag charged him, blazing white in the darkness. "No!" Finola screamed. "Stag, stop it!"

Her legs seemed too shaky to support her, but somehow the princess managed to struggle to the stag's side. He whirled at her approach, eyes so fierce that for one heartrending moment she thought he was going to attack *her*.

Then the wildness faded. The stag turned and melted into the night without a word, leaving Finola staring after him in confusion, pulling her cloak about herself with trembling hands.

"You should muzzle your pet," Fiain snarled. The princess turned sharply to him as he continued savagely, "Or make a rug of that ridiculous hide!"

Finola stared. Fiain lay sprawled in a graceless heap, the beautiful, scarred face twisted by fear and hatred into an ugly mask. So sudden a shudder of sheer revulsion shook the girl that she felt her stomach heave. Was *this* her gallant suitor? Gods, she'd let this—this vulgar, filthy *outlaw* kiss her, embrace her! Worse, she'd *wanted* him to!

Fighting the melodramatic urge to scrub her lips with a hand, not sure just then if she was angrier at him or at herself, Finola said shortly, "The stag was merely protecting me."

Fiain's only reply was a muttered curse.

"He won't hurt you," the princess continued. "J-just don't come near me again."

"No chance," he grumbled.

Finola didn't quite believe him. She wrapped her cloak more tightly about herself and sat in darkness, listening tensely for what seemed an eternity until Fiain's breathing finally steadied into a soft snoring.

But Finola couldn't have been farther from sleep. Touching her lips with a not-quite-steady hand, she couldn't keep from thinking about the strange, hot, thrill that had shot through her at the feel of Fiain's lips on hers. She had only wished to kiss someone—other than her father, of course (she would *not* think of Conal)—once before in her life, and that had been a quick, shy brush of lips between herself and Kiaran, a noble's son, back when they'd both been thirteen, the night before he'd had to return to his father's estates. She hadn't seen Kiaran since then. And no one else, of course, had ever dared kiss a princess.

Till now.

He's dangerous and dirty and—and I don't want anything to do with him!

Then why couldn't she quite believe it?

And what of the stag? Finola couldn't forget seeing how his eyes had fairly blazed with fury. Had that been merely a friend's anger, a friend's protection? Or . . . had she seen only the eyes of a . . . mindless beast?

Oh, dear gods, no!

Finola hugged her arms about her, blinking back sudden hot tears. Had she lost the stag? Had she lost her friend?

Soft, sweet breath touched her cheek. Finola sat bolt upright, hastily brushing her eyes dry. "Finola," the stag said quietly. "Don't be afraid. I'm still here."

"Why did you scare me like that?" she whispered fiercely. "Refusing to speak—I thought I'd lost you for good, and I—I couldn't bear—Why did you do it?"

"Och, I'm sorry."

"Sorry! You frighten me nearly to tears, and now you just say you're *sorry?*"

The stag looked as crestfallen as was possible for an animal. "I *am* sorry," he murmured. "I didn't mean to frighten you, truly. But I do not wish that one"—the sweep of antlers took in the restlessly sleeping Fiain—"to know I am anything more than a beast."

"But why?" Finola asked softly. "He can't possibly hurt you."

"Finola, I do not like his scent. He smells of—I don't have the human words. Of strangeness. Wrongness. Of not-to-be-trustedness. I tell you this, my friend: Be wary of him."

"Oh stag," Finola murmured, "we're going up against the Dark Druid. We're going to be challenging someone who may possibly be the most terrible sorcerer of our age, someone who wields the powers of the Outer Dark and will very likely crush us like two little insects. And you want me to worry about a simple human *outlaw?*"

"Just be wary," the stag repeated, and would say no more.

TEN

Experiments

"CLYWED MI! DYSGRU! UFUDDHAU!"

The sorcerous words blazed out, echoing and reechoing throughout Rhegeth's dark fortress. The small being that called itself Echi bit back a scream of terror at the fierce Power in them and curled itself more tightly into a corner, hugging thin arms about an equally thin body, shivering despite its coat of black fur.

Why, oh why, did the Master persist? Why did he keep trying—and after all these long years!—to dominate that beautiful, glittery box, that—that Gleaming Bright? When the spell failed, just as all the other spells the Master had used on the beautiful box had failed, the Master would be terrible in his rage. And, just as had happened before, he would surely take out that rage on poor, innocent Echi!

The little creature whimpered softly. It hadn't done anything wrong! Hadn't it always obeyed the Master? Done his bidding without a single argument? Brought him the box and—and—

The box. It all came down to that beautiful, beautiful box, that Gleaming Bright. Who would have thought such a glittery thing would lead to so much trouble?

"Ufuddhau! Ufuddhau!"

Aie, aie! There it was. The Master was losing his temper already, anger blazing in the Words of Command. Yes, aie, yes, and Echi could feel the wildfire crackle that meant unspent magic, useless magic, recoiling from the box in all directions. The little creature moaned in terror and tried to draw itself into a tighter curl yet, feeling its fur prickling as though lightning was about to strike.

Lightning, oh yes. With a wordless cry of rage, the Master rose from his throne-chair, dark robes swirling about him as he stalked away from the box on its plain black stand.

"Echi! *Echi!*"

It dared not resist the Master. None ever did. With a little wail of terror Echi uncurled, hurling itself submissively down at the Dark Druid's feet.

"Y-yes. Master? Is—is there anything the Master wishes from Echi?"

"You whimpering little fool." The contempt in the sorcerer's voice made Echi glance fearfully up. Rhegeth's eyes were flickering most terribly with anger. "Is *this* the best of my servants, *this?*"

"M-Master?"

"Be silent, worm!"

Echi knew the Master wasn't really mad at him. Echi knew the Master was only frustrated and angry at having all his spells fail to win control of the box's Power. But that didn't make it any easier to bear the sorcerous blows suddenly raining down on the creature from all sides.

After a timeless time of pain and terror, the blows slowed, then stopped, leaving Echi sobbing silently with relief. The Master stalked back to his throne-chair without a backwards glance and sat slumped, frowning, eyes hooded. Echi took advantage of the moment's quiet to drag itself off into the nice, safe shadows and lick its wounds, trying not to whimper at the soreness of its poor, bruised body.

What did Echi do wrong? Nothing! Nothing!

The creature stared bleakly into the darkness. Echi could remember no childhood, no time of being other than the way it was now. Long and long had it served the Master. This fortress had been all the home Echi could ever remember, all it had ever known.

Home, phaugh! It had overheard hunters talking longingly of home. Wasn't "home" supposed to be a nice, warm place of shelter? *This* was a place of—of existence, no more than that, a place of never knowing when an act, a word, a breath might spark the Master's rage. Surely other lives weren't like this?

What must it be like, Echi wondered dully, to be safe? To be *happy*?

Aie, aie, how did I ever come to such a pass?

Beaten for no reason yet never quite daring to leave; the world outside was a vast, unknown place of who knew what horrors. Here at least the horrors were known. Besides, a corner of the mind argued and argued that surely things would change, surely the Master would one day recognize Echi for a good, loyal servant and reward it and—and love it and . . . and . . .

And rot, Echi thought flatly. If such a marvel hadn't happened yet in all those years, it wasn't going to happen now. Staring into the darkness, the creature had nothing to look at but the truth: If it stayed, the beatings would continue. And one day they wouldn't stop in time. One day the Master would kill it.

No, Echi thought and again, *no. I will not let that happen.*

Oh, easy in the saying! Still, there must be some other place, some other Master who would appreciate poor Echi, who wouldn't hurt it for no reason at all.

I—I will not stay here, not any longer, Echi told itself, half-terrified at its own daring.

But surely such a daring thing was the only answer. Though no other servant of the Master had ever won freedom, though the Master's anger would be terrible if Echi was caught, this time, surely, would be different. Echi would *not* be caught. It would escape.

Yes, yes, the creature thought in growing excitement, Echi would at last be free!

Rhegeth had forgotten all about the little creature that served him. Slumped in his chair, too drained to move thanks to the aftereffects of sorcery expended in vain, the sorcerer stared at Gleaming Bright from beneath his half-lidded eyes.

What strange pseudolife was embedded in the very essence of the box? How could it possibly have the strength to resist the strongest spells Rhegeth had thrown at it down through the years? What manner of . . . monstrosity had Cathbad created?

"Curse you, old man," the sorcerer muttered, almost without heat. He found himself looking yet again—like a man who can't resist prodding an old wound even though he knows it will hurt him—back over the years to his days with Cathbad. Bah! What a maddening time that had been!

Most maddening, perhaps, because even when he'd been the rawest of apprentices, he had never once seen Cathbad lose his temper at him. Oh no, Cathbad had always been so *kind* to him, so *good*. So maddeningly, damnably superior!

Rhegeth stirred angrily. That was what truly rankled, even after all these years. No matter what he'd tried, no matter how much he had studied or how hard he had worked, somehow he'd never quite triumphed. Cathbad's spells had always been just that much finer than his, Cathbad's magic just that much more Powerful.

The Dark Druid let out his breath in an angry hiss. Frustration had finally overwhelmed him, back then, turning him tentatively towards the darker magics, just so he could at last have *something, anything* he could master better than Cathbad. Rhegeth's mouth tightened. It was almost humiliating to recall how foolish he'd been back then, half-afraid, not so much of what he was doing—though that had been, at least till he'd grown used to it, frightening enough—but that Cathbad would find him out. Ahh, but soon enough all fears had fled as he lost what he had been and gained what he was, as the soothing Darkness slid into his mind, his heart, as warmth and joy and Light lost their importance.

Your doing, Cathbad. I never would have left your pretty, clean path if only I'd been able to prove myself, just once, your better.

Except that Cathbad was still winning. Even now, dead of who knew how much old age, he was still managing to taunt his former pupil. Rhegeth glared in frustration at Gleaming Bright with its promise of immense Power—Power he so far couldn't even touch.

"Curse you, Cathbad," Rhegeth muttered again. "I will win."

But the smooth surface of Gleaming Bright remained smooth, unchanged, mocking him.

❧

Echi stole silently down corridors the creature knew only *seemed* to be empty, past twisted, demonic statues the creature knew only *seemed* to be lifeless. The Master neither needed nor wanted any other flesh-and-blood servants, but that didn't mean he and Echi were alone in the fortress. The little being glanced nervously back over its shoulder again and again, keeping strictly to the shadows even though it knew darkness wouldn't be a barrier to anything that might be watching.

But nothing stopped Echi. Heart pounding so rapidly its thin body shook, the creature squirmed its way out of a narrow window and scrabbled down the outer wall, long, skinny fingers and toes clinging desperately to the smallest depressions in the stone. Echi leaped the last few feet to the ground, glanced back once at the dark mass of fortress looming over it. Then, before the little being could lose courage, it raced with all its strength into the black, twisted forest ahead. Aie, but there was no good place to hide in this dead place, no friendly underbrush, nothing but the empty husks of trees.

I will keep running till I drop, yes, yes, or reach the nice, green forest beyond.

But there were limits. At last Echi slid to the ground in an exhausted little heap, gasping for breath. For a long while it lay still, waiting for strength to return.

Then the faintest creak of branches brought Echi bolt upright, staring wildly about. What? Where? Something was out there; something was stalking it! And if the hunter couldn't hide from Echi in this mockery of a forest, neither could Echi hide from the hunter—

There! Echi shrilled in terror at the sight of wild, blazing eyes and threw itself frantically to one side as the monster lunged. A heavy body went hurtling past it, landing with a vicious snapping and cracking of branches.

Now! Echi told itself. *Run!*

But the monster recovered too swiftly. Before Echi could so much as move, the thing was back on its feet, whirling on Echi, snarling. The little being shrieked anew at the sight of those long, long fangs and raced off into the forest, frantically darting this way, that.

The monster stayed right with it. Echi sobbed with fright, hearing those terrible snarls right behind it, feeling the monster's hot breath on its back.

And at last endurance ended, and Echi could run no more. Exhausted legs stumbled and set the little being crashing to the ground. As the monster loomed over it, Echi, despairing, knew this monstrous hunter was the Master's sending.

No one ever escaped the Master. No one.

ELEVEN

Monsters

CHUCKLING, FIAIN MOVED TO block Finola's path. "Sweetling, stop ignoring me."

Finola glared at him. "I'm not."

"Why, you haven't said more than a handful of words to me all day!" Fiain paused, grinning. "Was that your first kiss? Ha, yes, it *was*, wasn't it?"

Finola stepped around him and hurried on. "No. Of course not." *But I was never kissed by a grown man, a handsome, dangerous man—*There was not the slightest chance she was going to admit that to him! But Finola couldn't quite repress a little shiver, thinking of Conal and what *that* handsome, dangerous man had almost done to her.

Fiain, of course, misunderstood her shiver, and his grin deepened. "Was it such a terrible thing?" he prodded. "I could have sworn you were enjoying yourself."

Finola stopped short, hand on knife. "What happened, happened. It will *not* happen again!"

His smile was so superior she wanted to slap him. "Sweetling, you wound me to the heart."

"I'll wound you somewhere else if you so much as touch me again."

Fiain raised a thoughtful hand to his slashed cheek, and that smug smile faded ever so slightly. "You've already gone that way," he said softly. "Never again, my dear."

Nervously Finola started forward once more, half expecting Fiain to try to stop her again. But all he did was follow, keeping not quite close enough to her for her to complain about it, just close enough to keep her nerves on edge.

The stag had been ranging just ahead of them. Without warning, he halted, stiffening in alarm, head up, nostrils flaring.

"Now what?" Fiain muttered. "Smelled a wolf, did he?"

Ignoring the outlaw, Finola hurried to the stag's side, whispering, "What is it? I don't hear—"

"Not hear, *smell!*" The stag drew himself up to his full height, standing rigid as a silvery statue. "I'm right," he said, no longer even trying to whisper. "Something's coming, something terrible and fierce, though I don't know exactly what."

"Gods!" Fiain had moved to Finola's side, staring at the stag. "Gods! How are you doing that? I could swear the beast was talking!"

The stag glanced impatiently his way. "I *am* talking, man! Finola, hurry, we must—"

A terrified scream cut the air. A small, dark figure dashed through the forest in front of them—a child? Finola stared in disbelief. Could that possibly be a child alone in this foul place? A skinny little child wrapped in a coat of rough black fur?

A child being chased! Before Finola could shout a warning, a huge dark *thing,* all claws and fangs and hot, hating eyes, sprang out of the forest as though torn from the darkness, surging after the child. It bowled the slight figure over, whirling, diving to the kill.

"Fiain, do something!"

"Do what? Throw rocks at it?" the man asked wildly. "If we attract its attention, that monster's going to attack *us!* It's not as if we know the child or something."

Finola glanced at him in disgust. Snatching out her little leather hunting sling, she fit a smooth stone to it, took quick, careful aim, and let fly, hitting the monster with a sharp *thwack* on the side of its ugly head. The creature roared in startled pain and whirled to Finola, its eyes blazing molten yellow.

Oh gods.

"You see?" Fiain yelped. "Here it comes, *now!*"

But there was a sharp edge to his voice, almost of exultation. Before Finola could move, a rough shove sent her crashing to the ground, right into the monster's path. She scrambled to her feet, looking frantically about for the stag for help.

He's gone. They're both *gone, he and Fiain!*

Fiain, who'd just tried to kill her—and still

might succeed. Finola turned sharply back to the yellow-eyed beast as it charged. No time for a second stone; she didn't have a hope of outrunning the monster, either.

With the eerie calm that lies beyond fear, the princess did the only thing she could and stood her ground, hunting knife in hand. She was probably going to die here. The small blade wasn't going to be of much use against something that size. But at least, Finola thought defiantly, she was going to go down fighting!

Then the stag sprang out of the blackness like a white-hot flame. Roaring, head down, he charged the monster, sharp antlers slamming into it. With a fierce toss of his head, he hurled the heavy creature up, then sent it crashing to the forest floor. Still bellowing his fury, the stag stabbed at the monster again and again.

"Th-that's enough," Finola gasped. "Stag, that's enough! I—I think it's dead."

What if he wouldn't listen? What if his fury had finally pushed him all the way from speech to being nothing more than animal? Struggling with the terror trying to close her throat, Finola screamed, "Stop it! Stag, stop it! I told you, it's dead!"

She had to repeat that several times, but at last her words seemed to reach the stag's brain. He sprang back, panting and trembling, staring at the monster's torn, crumpled body, eyes so wide and wild the white showed all around their rims.

"It—it's all right," Finola soothed, struggling this

time with a voice that insisted on quivering. "Th-the creature's dead. What—whatever it was."

The stag blew hard, as though trying to clear his nostrils of the monster's stench, then rubbed his antlers savagely against the side of a tree to clean them. He turned to face Finola, and to her relief, she saw the mindless fury fade from those savage eyes.

"It would have killed you," the stag said wearily. "I couldn't let it kill you."

"Th-thank you. I . . ."

Suddenly Finola couldn't say another word. Instead, she rushed forward, throwing her arms about the stag's neck, hugging him, leaning against his warm side. For a moment the stag tensed in surprise, and the princess was sure he was going to toss her aside and run. But he only shivered once, then held himself rigidly still, letting Finola cling to him. After a moment, she felt his head lower to hers, his sweet breath (*like one of my father's cows or horses,* she thought) brushing softly at her face. His nose touched her cheek ever so lightly, tickling, and Finola gave a shaky laugh and backed away.

"L-let's get away from here."

"Fiain." The stag spat out the name. "Where is he?"

"Still running, probably." Finola swallowed drily, remembering the feel of those strong hands pushing her in front of charging death. No, no, he couldn't have meant to kill her, part of her mind yammered, not after that kiss; he must have panicked the way cowards panicked, mindlessly trying to get anything at all between them and danger.

Wonderful. That makes him either a coward or a would-be murderer.

She would *not* think of him again, Finola resolved, she would *not!* The weak, sly, perilous creature wasn't worth the waste of a single thought! She'd forget him and everything about him and think only of Gleaming Bright and a happy ending to this stupid quest. "Ah, but the child! I forgot about—*He's* gone, too!"

"A child is a human fawn?" the stag asked warily.

"Yes, of course."

"Then that was not a child."

"But—"

"It had nothing of baby scent about it, nothing of *human* scent about it."

"But I—you—it—" Finola broke off in confusion, then exploded, "The sooner we get out of this hideous forest—"

"The happier we shall both be."

The princess took a deep breath. "You . . . don't have to go on."

"I will not stay *here!*"

"That's not what I meant." *I don't want to say this, I don't!* Forcing her words out, Finola continued reluctantly, "You saved my life. You did. The debt is paid." She swallowed drily. "Th-that makes you free to go your way."

"My way," the stag said grimly, "is with you."

"Oh, that's ridiculous! You hate being here,

you're so scared your skin shivers! Get out of here!
Go home!"

*Oh, isn't this fine. Now I sound like I'm shooing
away a stray dog!*

"No," the stag told her.

"Yes!" If she stopped now, Finola knew she was
going to burst into tears, so she continued fiercely,
"You're acting like a fool! Like some fool of a human hero who hasn't the sense to—"

"I am not a human. And I do not understand
this word you use, this . . . hero."

She gave a wordless cry of frustration. The stag
said quietly, "Finola, you are brave as a doe defending her fawn. But you've just shown me you
cannot survive alone."

Was he thinking of the monstrous beast or of
Fiain? "Nonsense," the princess muttered. "Stag, I
don't want you to get hurt. It wouldn't be fair, it
wouldn't be right, and I—don't think I could
stand it. You don't even understand what all this
stupid hunting is about!"

"Why should I understand human things?" the
stag said, so sensibly she wanted to hit him. "But
I know this: A stag does not abandon a doe. I
shall not abandon my human friend."

"But you can't—"

"That," the stag told her firmly, "is that."

"But—"

"No. Now, come." He gave Finola a shove with
his head, nearly knocking her over. "Go on. Go!
The faster we travel, the sooner we are free of
here."

With a sigh, Finola surrendered. "Thank you," she murmured, trying not to show her relief. As they moved on, she added thoughtfully, "I just wonder what happened to that child—Yes, yes, I know it wasn't really a child. But I do wonder what happened to that . . . that poor, frightened little whatever-it-was. I wonder if we'll ever find out."

❧

Wild with panic, Echi raced blindly through the Master's forest, feeling the world, the very world turning aslant, spilling out its logic. The monster had been terrible, all fierce claws and hatred, but that hatred had been understandable, logical, the Master's hatred. Disobedience meant death, of course it did, the Master made it so. And even though Echi hadn't wanted to die, it had accepted what must be—

But then, without warning, death was gone, death was slain, and Echi's life was given back and—and *why? Why?* It made no sense! The strangers, the strangers had killed the Master's hatred-made-flesh—but *why?* Why had they done it? Why save Echi? Why risk their own lives? No one did that! No one risked a life without a goal; no one helped another save for gain! The strangers didn't even know Echi! What did they *want* of it? What did they *want?*

There is only the Master who gives life or death! There cannot be another! The little being wailed aloud, a long, thin stream of sound, and continued to run. *Too much strangeness. I cannot bear more strangeness, I—I—I cannot!*

It was far beyond poor Echi's bearing, yes. Echi would go home, back to the Master, back to where at least it *knew* what to find, what to expect. There would be cruelty, yes, but at least with the Master the world would not tilt, the logic would not change. There would be no more of this chaotic, unbearable, terrifying *kindness!*

TWELVE

Journey's End

THE BOY CRINGED AGAINST *the shack's plank
wall, trying to hide his thin body in the shadows cast
by the one smoky lantern, struggling not to move or
breathe or do anything at all that might draw attention
to himself. For what seemed like ages Dunod had sat
drinking and drinking, slumped over the table like a
big, dark bear, muttering broken bits and pieces of
curses as he always did, complaining about the Law
that wouldn't let a man do his job.*

*His job. Dunod's job was whatever anyone looking
for brute strength would pay him to do. He'd given the
boy shelter when no one else had, and enough scraps
of food to keep him alive—just so he'd have someone
to do the dirty bits of a job for him: the spying out of
danger, the luring of the chosen target into danger,
the searching of a dead man's clothing for whatever
might be used or sold.*

The boy shuddered. He'd even, when Dunod insisted, helped strip off that clothing if it was of good quality, and sold it to old Fychan, who dealt in used goods and didn't ask questions.

Dunod's cursing was getting louder. The boy bit his lip and did his best to act like only part of the wall, the earthen floor. Lately jobs had been far and few, and the targets so poor they'd not been worth hitting. When Dunod got like this, filling his belly with drink instead of food, he took out his anger on whoever came too close.

If he hits me again, I'll kill him. Terrified by his daring, the boy repeated the silent vow anyhow. If Dunod hit him or did any of the . . . the other things to him, the boy would kill him.

"You. Boy. C'mere."

If I ignore him, maybe he'll forget about me.

Not a chance. "Damn you," Dunod roared, "I said, come here!"

Heart racing, the boy got to his feet. "What is it?"

"Don't you give me that 'what is it' garbage!" A rough hand caught the boy's arm, dragging him to the table. "When I call you, you jump, unnerstand?"

Dry-mouthed, the boy nodded. It wasn't enough. Without warning, Dunod released him, backhanding him across the face, sending him staggering back against the wall. Dunod got unsteadily to his feet, towering over the boy, eyes glittering in the uncertain lantern light.

"Told'ya not to gimme that 'I'm too good for you' look." His blow sent the boy tumbling to the floor.

"I didn't mean—"

"Didn't mean—Don't gimme none of that garbage!"

Before the boy could scramble aside, Dunod dragged him to his feet again. "Teach you a lesson. Teach you a good lesson."

Dunod pulled a ragged length of rope from the wall, letting go of the boy to test it with a smack against his palm. "Yeah," he muttered with a dark grin. "A good lesson."

He's going to kill me, *the boy knew with sudden horror.* This time Dunod wasn't going to stop with just a beating. This time he's going to kill me.

As the first blow came whistling down, the boy darted aside, sobbing with fright.

"Hold still, you li'l—"

The rope smacked down again, hitting the boy a glancing blow that sent him crashing against the table. Desperately he snatched up the first thing that came to hand—

The lantern! As Dunod charged him, the boy hurled the smoky thing with all his might. To his horrified fascination, it broke over Dunod's drink-sodden hair and beard, and flame roared up. Dunod screamed, screamed, screamed—

And Rhegeth awoke, his own terrified screams still echoing in his ears, to find himself alone in the quiet darkness of his keep.

A dream.

A foul dream, tormenting him just as if he were some plain, magicless man. Ridiculous.

After a moment, his breathing steadied. Rhegeth got slowly to his feet, looking blankly about his somber bedchamber, his mind still taunting him with wisps of memory. There really had been a

Dunod; there really had been a boy, himself, lost and desperate enough to—

No. What had happened had happened so many years ago, long before he'd run off to Cathbad. Why dream of it now?

Why, indeed? The Dark Druid frowned. Could some arcane inner sense possibly have been sending him a warning? Of what? Suddenly uneasy, Rhegeth threw on his clothes and stalked down the long, silent corridors. Somewhere outside the keep, he sensed, it was full day, but mere time meant little to him; the Dark Druid ate or slept when it pleased him and kept himself swathed in soothing darkness.

A flick of will lit the nearest candelabra; his night-sighted eyes needed no more light than that. A second flick of will brought a soundless servant (not Echi, not the would-be runaway still nursing its new bruises somewhere in a corner, but a blank-eyed grayish man-thing) with a ewer of pure water. Rhegeth took the ewer and waved the servant away without even glancing the creature's way. Filling the smooth silver bowl he used for his scrying, the Dark Druid set about quieting his mind, soothing his thoughts, murmuring the Words to bring his senses to sharpest focus.

Now.

As he studied it, the water stirred, shimmered, darkened, then stilled once more, now turned smooth and glassy as a mirror. Rhegeth permitted himself the faintest nod of satisfaction, then bent over the bowl, staring into it as though staring through a small, round window, peering at something hovering just at the edge of sight.

Somewhere out there lurked whatever had disturbed him . . . somewhere, his senses told him, in the black, sorcerous forest. . . . Rhegeth sighed softly. The aura of his own sorcery blanketing that forest interfered with his psychic sight the way fog might interfere with physical sight. But if he focused all his will, he could still make out enough . . . just . . . barely . . . enough . . .

So-o, was *that* it? Rhegeth straightened in surprise. Had the fool actually dared return?

But . . . was that someone at the fool's side? The Dark Druid stared and stared till eyes and mind ached, then let out his breath in an angry hiss. He could see nothing more than fog and fog and cursed fog!

So be it. If he couldn't see clearly, Rhegeth decided, his smile thin and cold, at least he could do this one thing: make that fool regret ever trying to defy him.

øª·

"Are you still thinking of that man?" the stag asked suddenly, and Finola started guiltily.

"Fiain? No. Yes . . . I guess I am."

The stag shook his antlered head. "Humans are strange. He is . . . what is the word? Fine-formed?"

"Handsome."

"Ah. He is handsome for a human, yes?"

"Oh yes."

"And proud of being handsome. But you marked

him." The stag paused thoughtfully. "When a stag is left scarred after a fight, he accepts what has happened. It means little to him, so long as he may still lead his life as it is meant to be lived. But humans don't accept so simply?"

Finola sighed. "No, they don't. All right, then, maybe he was angry at me for scarring his face. But that doesn't mean—"

The stag gave a great sigh. "From what you've told me of that first meeting, you shamed him in the eyes of his—his herd. You made him look like a feeble little fawn."

"I—Oh. I did, didn't I?" After all, the only pride an outlaw could possibly have left would be in his control over his fellows. And here she'd come, not even a trained warrior but "just a girl," as he'd so lightly called her, to take away even that.

He must, all along, have hated her, subtly, slyly—Curse it, she was *not* going to start weeping! So what if Fiain had hidden his true feelings for her! What else had she expected? That he would turn out to be a prince in disguise who would carry her off to—

Bah, ridiculous!

Fiain had been out only for revenge or whatever treasure she might lead him to. As it had happened, the chance for revenge had come first. Those were the facts, and that was an end to it. Finola stared grimly ahead, refusing to grant him even one tear.

But then Finola stared, and stared again, feeling

the first faint stirrings of hope. Surely it was lighter up ahead than before? Could that actually be normal, natural daylight?

Please, please let it be!

She hurried forward, the stag loping lightly at her side, then let out a little whoop of relief. "Oh yes, it is daylight! We're almost out of the forest, and . . . stag? What is it? What's wrong?"

The stag had stopped short, shuddering visibly. "We are now so very near *his* keep. There . . ."

Finola gingerly parted two thorny bushes, their branches cracking drily at her touch, and found herself looking out at daylight: a gray, ugly world of an overcast sky and a jagged hill. . . .

As she saw what loomed on that hill, a chill weight settled within her. *Gods, and to think I was worrying over someone as . . . trivial as Fiain!*

Finola had been steeling herself for this moment from the day she'd left Irwain. But oh, she had never expected Rhegeth's keep to look *quite* this dark, *quite* this ugly! A great mound of stone, it rose out of the forest like some grisly, brooding beast of prey.

And I have to find Gleaming Bright in all that?

"I can't," the stag murmured. "I—I—I can't go on."

Finola glanced his way, then put a gentle hand on his shoulder, feeling the tremors shaking him. "Ah, stag, don't be afraid," she soothed, even though her own heart was racing in panic. "It's just a building, not—"

"You . . . do . . . not . . . do not . . . understand!" The stag rolled a white-rimmed glance her way, forcing out the words. "I . . . c-can't . . . go on!"

Oh gods, he meant it literally. It wasn't just that he was sensing the sorcerous aura, terrifying though that must be to an animal (*and to me!* Finola admitted). No, no, the dark force was affecting the magic, talking side of him as well! Finola bit her lip. What if he lost the power to speak at all? What if he lost all signs of intelligence because of her?

Maybe he'd be happier that way, an animal like every other animal—

No, oh no, he was *himself,* a separate, witty, charming being, and if he was destroyed for her sake—

"N-never mind," Finola said. "You don't have to go on. It's my hunt, after all. Stay here, stag. I can go on alone."

"No!"

"Yes."

The stag gave a great roar of anguish. "I cannot help you!"

"Hush. You've already helped me."

Finola forced herself forward, but the wild-eyed stag blocked her way. "Stag, don't—"

"Listen to me!" he gasped. "I . . . was . . . I was here before! I know it! And . . . and . . . I . . . know . . . here . . . you . . ." He shook his antlered head impatiently. "Memory . . . something of . . . 'if one of . . . of pure heart and . . . resolve' . . . I *can't!*"

"Are you saying," Finola asked dubiously, "that the only way to get in there is to be pure of heart and resolve?"

The stag said nothing.

"Well, I . . . uh . . . don't know how pure my heart is"—she would *not* think of Fiain—"but if I've come this far, I certainly don't intend to stop now, so I guess that fills the 'resolve' requirement. Ha, it probably just means Rhe—ah, *that one* has his defense spells set for such strong menaces, like soldiers or other sorcerers. They can't be triggered by one magicless, unarmed—Wait, now. Spells are one thing. But how am I going to get past his guards?"

Finola frowned, staring at the fortress intently. "Wherever they are. Someone should be patrolling the walls, but I don't see a soul anywhere. He . . . does *have* guards, doesn't he? He must. It hardly seems possible for even a sorcerer not to have—But then, nothing about this journey has ever seemed possible, and—Och, I'm babbling."

The princess took a great breath, then let it out slowly, trying to calm her racing heart. "If I wait any longer, I'll never have the courage to move. Stag, I—I'm going. I'll be back, with—with what I'm hunting."

Somehow.

I hope.

THIRTEEN

Questing

FINOLA CREPT TOWARDS THE fortress, as flat to the ground as she could manage, moving bit by careful bit, trying not to make a sound, hardly daring even to breathe. The great dark walls began to loom over her, looking more and more vast as she neared them till they seemed to shut out the sky.

But I still don't see anyone on those walls. I don't see any guards at all!

Finola hesitated a moment, then scrambled to her feet. Hunched over just in case somebody *was* lurking up there, sure she was going to hear a shout as she was spotted, she scurried up to the walls of the *dun*, diving into their shadow. Ugh, the stones were cold and clammy! Finola snatched her hand away, looking cautiously about.

The gate's wide open, as though Rhegeth didn't have a care in the world! But then, who was going to be paying a visit to a Dark Druid? *Idiotic questers like me, that's who. But there still doesn't seem to be anyone else around.*

Did she dare? *No,* Finola admitted. But she couldn't just stand here forever, either.

Heart pounding so fiercely she thought she was going to be sick, the princess edged forward. The *dun's* gateway was huge, flanked by two of the ugliest stone monsters the most warped of carvers could ever have created. An eerie mix of lion, bear, human, and she wasn't sure what else, they sat back on powerful haunches, their muscular, claw-tipped paws and fang-filled, snarling mouths looking alarmingly real. Finola peered beyond them, into the fortress, but could see only darkness. She glanced up at the statues and licked her suddenly dry lips.

They really were skillfully carved, so much so that she could almost imagine them turning those ugly stone heads to look down at her. But that wasn't possible . . . was it? Surely they weren't . . . alive?

Oh, nonsense. Feeling greatly daring, the princess rapped one of them with her fist. Nothing happened. *Of course not, you idiot! They're ugly as hate, but they're only stone.*

Finola slid warily past them, not quite brave enough to ignore them altogether, then stopped short at the entrance itself. If only it wasn't *quite* so dark in there! And if only she had a torch!

Why not ask for a trumpet as well, to let everyone know exactly where I am?

Was she going to stand dithering out here till Rhegeth came to get her? Gathering her courage, Finola dove into the darkness, then waited in terrified impatience for her eyes to adjust, listening with all her might to silence that seemed far too dense to be natural.

At last, to Finola's immense relief, she could see again, however faintly. Now that her eyes had gotten used to the gloom, she realized that the fortress wasn't totally black after all; Finola couldn't tell the exact source of the light, but, peering through the dimness, she saw that it was lit—after a fashion—by the faintest, eeriest hint of a glow. Rhegeth, sorcerer or no, was apparently still human enough to need *some* light.

Not that there was much to see. As Finola tiptoed forward, she found that the main entranceway ran straight into the fortress for perhaps half a hundred paces, then branched off into the openings of a true maze of corridors. She glanced into one, then another, in growing confusion. Which way now? There wasn't a clue as to where any of them led; all the corridors were equally bare.

Doesn't Rhegeth like any comforts? This looks more like an animal's den—no, no, like an insect hive, all clean and weird and sterile—than a human's fortress!

Here and there lurked more of the ugly, monstrous, all too realistic statues, smaller ones this time that fit neatly into the corridors, hiding in corners or leaning casually against walls as though they were just waiting for the Dark Druid's spell to bring them to life. Finola stole past those standing in the main corridor—twisted, muscular creatures with scales and wings—her nerves prickling, sure she could hear the faintest groaning of stone as if the statues were turning their heads to watch her pass.

Och, no, of course they weren't moving. Nothing here was moving but she. Maybe Rhegeth, in his pride, really did depend only on his sorceries to keep him safe; maybe his defensive spells really were set against magical beings or armies, not against something as minor as one unarmed, magicless girl.

Or maybe he was just playing with her, like a palace cat with a mouse that only thought it could escape without—No, she was *not* going to start thinking like that!

Which way do I go, though? I can't just wander about at random. Finola glanced helplessly from corridor entrance to corridor entrance, seeing no differences between them. If she didn't make a decision quickly, the princess knew, she was going to lose what was left of her nerve and turn and run. *How can I possibly find Gleaming Bright in all this tangle?*

But the box was supposed to be powerfully magical, and designed to be used only by her family. Surely it would be weary of captivity? Surely it would want her to find it?

Oh, ridiculous. I don't care how magical it is, a box can't want anything!

Still . . . Ah well, ridiculous or not, it was worth a try. "Hear me, Gleaming Bright," Finola whispered into the darkness. "Cathbad gave you to King Donal and his kin. I am Donal's descendant, his granddaughter, heir to the throne."

She turned this way and that, listening, sniffing the dank air, trying to find even the vaguest hint of a clue. It had been stupid even to think that a box would—

Odd . . . turning towards the corridor farthest to the left somehow felt marginally more comfortable, though she couldn't exactly figure out why. Imagination? Finola shrugged slightly and started down the left-hand corridor. This might not be the wisest choice, but it was better than no choice at all.

る

A small patch of darkness stirred, uncurled, became Echi, staring in suddenly awakened curiosity. An intruder? An actual intruder? There had never been one, not one who'd blithely passed the entrance-spells and lived, not in all the years Echi could remember. Who was this? Who dared come here? The little being cautiously stretched its skinny arms and legs, wincing at its bruises, then padded silently after the intruder.

Ah, now Echi saw who it was, and gave the softest hiss of surprise. So, and so and so! This was the young human, the girl, the one who had helped Echi, the one who had saved it from the Master's beast. But what was she doing here? Not for Echi to question, no, no, Echi should surely

obey its orders, run to rouse the Master, tell him
of this intruder.

But, why? Echi froze, stunned by its own daring.
But: Why, indeed? What had such obedience ever
earned it before but bruises?

Aie, aie, but there would be worse than bruises
if the Master learned it had not instantly obeyed!

But . . . this young human had saved Echi. She
had shown Echi . . . kindness, frightening but
wonderful. If the Dark Druid was awakened, there
would be an end to kindness. Yet if the Dark
Druid did not wake, and learned later of the intruder, there might be an end to Echi!

Yes, but . . . kindness, that one brief sense of
warmth, of another actually caring . . . The little
being shivered in confusion, trying to think things
out, biting back tiny, frightened whimpers. It had
never had to choose like this, never!

At last Echi slowly straightened to its full slight
height, terrified and amazed at its own defiance. *I
choose "no,"* it decided. *I will* not *wake the Master.
Not yet.*

It would wait, and watch, and follow. And
maybe somehow all would fit together and work
out well.

Heedless, the girl wandered on. Soundless as the
darkness around it, Echi followed.

૨ª

How long had she been walking? Finola shook her
head: impossible to keep track of time in all this
dim sameness. All she could do was keep following

the faint whims or magics or whatever they were that led her this way and that.

Maybe, she thought wearily, *there isn't a way out of this tangle of corridors. Maybe Rhegeth put a spell on me and I didn't even know it. Maybe he means for me to just keep on wandering till I drop dead from hunger or exhaustion.*

There still wasn't another living thing to be seen, not even the tiniest of the vermin that usually inhabited a fortress, mice or fleas. By now the endless silence was hurting her ears and nerves so much that Finola had to battle against the urge to scream just so she'd hear *some* human sound.

And wouldn't that be a stupid thing! Why not just yell for Rhegeth while I'm at it and—Oh.

The passage she was following had suddenly come to an end. Beyond lay a vast chamber weakly lit by the stubs of thick candles, half-smothered by their own melting wax and set in huge, heavy candlesticks shaped to look like grotesque figures. The flickering light made the figures seem to writhe, shrieking in endless, silent terror, and Finola shuddered.

But then her breath caught in her throat. There at the far end of the chamber, in a great, throne-like chair, sat a shrouded, dark-robed figure that could only be Rhegeth, the Dark Druid.

And there was no way he could have missed seeing her.

FOURTEEN

Dark Perils

RHEGETH SAT IN SILENT grandeur, a quiet, menacing darkness made all the darker by contrast with the strange golden glow that seemed to be coming from beyond his left shoulder.

For a long, terrified while, Finola couldn't so much as move, sure she was dead, waiting helplessly for some horrible spell to strike her down. But Rhegeth stirred. At last, holding her breath, the princess took a wary step forward, then another, nerves prickling. Surely now . . . ?

Nothing happened. Finola moved delicately closer and closer yet. Och, what—To her horror, she heard the faintest of rhythmic rumbles surround the sorcerer. Gods, had she roused some protective spell? Was she about to—

No! Finola just barely smothered a panicky laugh. Snoring! The Dark Druid was snoring!

Rhegeth must have been working some spell so powerful it exhausted him.

Knowing that, Finola reminded herself, wasn't getting her to Gleaming Bright. She still felt that strange urge telling her she was headed the right way, perilous though that way might be. Och, well, so be it: why should things be different now?

Finola started to tiptoe warily past the sleeping sorcerer, then froze with a startled, involuntary little gasp. There to Rhegeth's left was a small stand. And on it rested the source of the glow: a box that could only be Gleaming Bright. It was far smaller than she'd imagined, but glinted and glittered with its own light like a little, living sun, brightening a ring of darkness about it.

Wonderful, oh wonderful . . .

Stupid to stand here gawking! Finola hastily roused herself and tiptoed forward again, forced to pass so close to the Dark Druid that she could clearly see the cruel, harsh lines of Rhegeth's face beneath the dark hood, lit by the glitter from Gleaming Bright. Oh gods, if he woke now . . .

But he never stirred. Holding her breath, terrified that the sorcerer's eyes were going to suddenly snap open, Finola reached past him and snatched up the box. For a moment she hesitated again, startled by its lightness. A groan from Rhegeth made her start. Oh gods—

No. He was still asleep, dreaming. But what if the dream woke him? Clutching Gleaming Bright to her, Finola hurried back out of the chamber and down the maze of corridors, trying to move as quietly as a breeze, until she had left the Dark Druid far behind.

At last, panting and shaky legged, she had to stop. Struggling to catch her breath, hardly believing what she'd done, Finola looked down at the box clutched in her arms. How beautiful it was— but how strange! Gleaming Bright did appear to be solid gold. (But how? her mind yammered. Gold was heavy! Even so small a golden box couldn't possibly be so light!) Every bit of it, sides and top, was engraved in graceful, intricate patterns that confused her eyes when she tried to study them.

But it really *was* small, hardly larger than her jewel box back at home. How could something so little and light possibly hold anything magical—or, indeed, anything at all?

What if Rhegeth's spells have done something to it? What if he has destroyed its powers, and all this was for nothing?

Oh, terrible thought! Licking dry lips, the princess opened Gleaming Bright's lid a cautious crack and peeked inside.

Dear gods!

She wasn't looking into its interior at all! No, no, she was staring, as though through a tiny window, at a face, a man's face. Fiain? No, definitely not. Whoever this was, he was far younger than Fiain, maybe a few years her senior at the most, his hair the type of pale blond that tended to bleach nearly white in summer. His face wasn't at all handsome, but Finola, considering, thought she rather liked it anyhow: the sort of face that came pleasantly to life when its owner was smiling.

He was certainly far from smiling now. His dark brown eyes, startling against the fair skin and hair, were so sad that Finola felt a tiny pang of pity, then frowned in confusion. Who was this? And why—

And why am I being foolish enough to stand here and gape? Whoever he is, the mystery can wait!

Just because things had gone remarkably well so far (almost as though Gleaming Bright really had wanted her here, really had, somehow, been smoothing her path) didn't mean they'd continue that way. Finola hastily shut the box and hurried on.

Ha, who would have expected this? Rhegeth's ugly statues were helping her! His sculptor had done too good a job, carving no two exactly alike, and so she remembered this corridor because of its two bat-winged statues, one stiff-backed, the other bent; and this bend of the following corridor because of the snarling, crouching, three-horned whatever-it-was; then down this way to the right . . . Yes, yes, thank you, Rhegeth, she might actually find her way back out of this maze!

But that uneasy sense of being watched was still with her, stronger than before. And with every step she took, Finola was sure she heard the faintest hint of scrapings and slitherings behind her. . . .

Don't look back, she told herself sharply. *Just keep moving. That's all. Just keep moving.*

Echi had stood unnoticed at the chamber door, watching as the girl approached the Master, wondering with pounding heart if she was mad enough to wake him. Echi had watched, too, astonished, when she'd reached smoothly past the sleeping Master to steal away Gleaming Bright. That was when it should have shouted, the little being told itself sharply, yes, yes, that was when it should surely have shouted to wake the Master.

And yet, and yet . . . all the endless years of loneliness and pain seemed to be filling its mind . . . all the endless years of the Master's cruelty or simple, cold indifference. . . . How dark Echi's life had seemed till now, how oh so painfully lonely against the one quick flash of light the girl had given it, the warmth of that true concern, that saving of Echi and worry about its safety and— and—

Echi smiled thinly in a flicker of small, sharp teeth. The golden box had brought it nothing but pain. The human girl seemed able to handle it. Let her have it!

And yet . . . its mind, conditioned well by Rhegeth, insisted this was treason, treason. . . .

But the Master was pain, the girl was warmth. *I don't know what to do!* Echi wailed silently. Trembling with confusion, it followed the girl down the dark, winding corridors like a small, soundless scrap of night, praying that someone else would help it, make the decision for it.

All about it, Echi sensed, the sorcerous statues

were stirring into pseudo-life, dimly aware in their cold stone beings that a theft had been committed against their creator, and the little being whimpered in growing alarm. It had no sorcerous abilities; it certainly didn't have the power to lull the statues back to sleep. This was the last, the worst, the cruelest of the Master's games: let any thief who could steal this far think all was well, simple, easy; then, the moment that thief tried to escape . . .

Oh, Echi knew only too well what happened then. Had it not watched the Master set the spells? No thief, no matter how bold, could be totally calm in such a place. And so the spells would start, most subtly, to play upon human fears, slyly, subtly, working that fear into a frenzy, taking bits of terror from the thief's brain and hurling them back. At last, of course, the thief would have to look back—and in looking back, rouse the statues into full, terrible life!

Echi quivered in an agony of suspense. Maybe the golden box would protect the girl, shield her from the worst of that perilous terror. But she still might look; she still might die! "Be wary!" Echi whispered sharply, hoping the human girl would hear, praying she would heed, but not daring to make too much noise. "Whatever you see or hear, *do not look back!*"

❧

Finola froze, listening with all her might.

"Do not look back!"

Had she heard it? Was that faintest whisper real, or some sorcerous trick?

Whatever it is, I am not going to stop to find out!

Gleaming Bright seemed just as eager to get out of this dark place as she, brightening or dimming every time she made a turn, as though doing its best to help guide her.

But oh, the maze of corridors seemed endless! And now she could definitely hear the hissings and slitherings and creakings of stone growing louder, no doubt about it, coming up just behind her, closing in all around her. . . .

Finola bit back a terrified sob. No wonder it had been so simple to get into the fortress! Rhegeth didn't care who got *in;* he simply wasn't going to let them *out* again. *She* was never going to get out of here, never; she was going to be crushed by living stone or buried alive in all this darkness, she and Gleaming Bright both; she was never going to see light again. . . .

Ha, no, wait! That *was* light up ahead, no matter how faint, brighter than this eternal vague gloom—yes, that was definitely daylight! She was nearly out of here; she was nearly free—

Something suddenly caught the end of her cloak and brought her up short.

No, oh no, not now, not so close to freedom!

With a wild cry of despair, Finola whirled to face her attacker.

FIFTEEN

Trapped

DEEP IN HIS SLEEP, Rhegeth stirred restlessly, dreaming . . .

He was watching his own life pass before him as though it was a performance, seeing himself travel far, from helpless, bitter, tormented boy to frustrated apprentice-magician to full, darkness-filled sorcerer, feeling the fear in him grow, then fade, then change to coldness as his Power grew.

Ah yes, the Power, the magic that was all, the only important thing in his life, the gathering of more and more Power . . . wonderful, wonderful. And with the thought of ever-increasing Power, the dream began shifting from reality into pleasant, pleasant fantasy. . . .

Yes, ah yes, now he found himself master of all Power. Now he found himself ruling a vast, sorcerous realm stretching from world's edge to world's edge, controlling it all from his solitary, terrible fortress. Every being within that realm feared him, worshiped him, obeyed his merest whim. And Cathbad's spirit, bound helpless within a tiny silver cage, cringed and fawned at his approach, admitting that Rhegeth was his ruler, Rhegeth was the mightiest sorcerer ever. . . .

But suddenly the faintest quiver of uneasiness quivered through the dream, the smallest sense of something not quite right, something not quite belonging.

A thief. A thief had stolen into his fortress.

"No matter," Rhegeth's sleeping self murmured coolly. "He will not survive."

But the thief had managed to worm his way so very far within the fortress; the thief had managed to worm his way even here, into this very chamber—

"Impossible."

And yet now the thief was stealing away his source of strength. The thief was stealing away Gleaming Bright!

No. That could not be. He was dreaming, the Dark Druid was dimly aware of it now, all this was only dreaming.

But his sorcery stirred within that dream, sending out delicate webs of magic to find, search, puzzle out the mind of the thief, teasing out bits of memories . . . yes, and yes . . . easy for that one to enter this fortress, difficult, so difficult to leave. . . .

And so, in sleep, traps were set and armed and altered. . . .

With a wild cry of despair, Finola whirled to face her attacker—and froze in astonishment.

"*Fiain!*"

Oh, but how piteously changed he was! Few traces of the dangerous, beautiful outlaw remained: his golden hair hung in lank, matted strings about his shoulders; his clothing was little more than filthy rags; and his once-elegantly fair face, marked by the thin red line of the scar, was gaunt and streaked with dirt.

His eyes were those of a tortured beast.

"Help me," Fiain gasped, reaching feebly out to her, "please, please, sweetling, help me. . . ."

Finola suddenly realized she was clutching Gleaming Bright to her so tightly her fingers ached, and relaxed her grip ever so slightly. "What are you *doing* here?"

"Got here before you . . . thought this surely had to be where you were headed."

"Yes, but—"

"Treasure, I thought," he murmured with the thin ghost of a grin, "had to be wondrous treasure in such a place. . . ." He shook his head. "Treasure. Never realized a sorcerer lived here."

"Then why did you . . ."

Fiain shrugged painfully. "I was a fool. Even knowing what *he* was, I still thought I could get the better of *him*, rob *him*. That was a bad mistake, very bad. *He* caught me." The man shivered, cringing back like a hurt, frightened child. "*He* plays with my mind, Finola, makes me see things, do things. Suffer things. Ah please, sweetling, I—I can't stand his games any longer. Free me or—or kill me."

Kill him! "No!" Finola gasped. "Fiain, look, the gateway out of this place is right there." But then she paused, a chill little shiver stealing along her spine at his blank, wild stare. "C-can't you see it?"

He turned that wild stare to her. "Sweetling, don't jest with me. I see nothing there but blackness."

"But it's—Come, follow me, I'll show you."

She started towards the light, but Fiain called piteously after her, "Wait!" Finola turned to see he hadn't moved at all. "I can't . . . can't escape," he said softly. "*He* won't let me."

Bits of memory flashed through her mind: Fiain in his ragged beauty . . . Fiain kissing her, his arms strong about her . . . Fiain sending that strange, unfamiliar fire through her.

Of course. And Fiain pushing her into the path of the rushing monster. Fiain trying to kill her. She wasn't going to be foolish about this.

But . . . the look in those tortured eyes . . . the eyes that had been so beautiful . . .

I can't leave him here, no matter what he did. "How can I help you?" Finola asked.

"Take my hand."

"What—"

"Please, just take my hand. The touch of your unsorcelled flesh will break *his* hold on me."

"I . . ."

"Please! Either that, or kill me! I—I can bear no more!"

"Shh! You'll wake Rhe—ah, *him.*" Hastily Finola reached out a hand and felt Fiain's fingers close about it—rough fingers that suddenly seemed to have a crushing force in them. "Let go!" Finola gasped. "Fiain, you're hurting me! Fiain—"

But it was Fiain no longer. As Finola stared in horror, she saw the last hint of him, the wild, tormented eyes, fade into the flat, empty eyes of a stone statue. A statue monstrous as a scaly, bat-winged demon that, most horribly, moved with false life.

"No . . ."

The princess fought frantically to free her hand, but the stone hand held it fast no matter how she struggled. A deep creaking and groaning of stone sent thrills of new horror through her. More of the statues were moving towards her, moving to grasp and hold and crush.

A trick, it was all a trick! Gleaming Bright! I have to—

To what? How did she call on its magic? As Finola fumbled with Gleaming Bright, one-handed, a second stony hand struck her arm a glancing blow. The box flew from her grip, crashing with such force to the floor that Finola screamed, "No!"

If it had been damaged, if its magic had been destroyed, she was lost! Finola managed to twist free before the hand could close on her shoulder, but her hand was still trapped in the grip of the first statue; she couldn't quite reach the box no matter how she strained. Gleaming Bright didn't seem to have been damaged by the fall, but it had landed with lid slightly ajar.

I opened it to see that vision of—of whoever he was; raising the lid has to be part of the spell—

Praying that a mere opening like that was enough to spark its magic, Finola gasped out, "Gleaming Bright, hear me. I'm of Donal's blood, you—you know that. In Cathbad's name, help me!"

Nothing happened.

Wait, wait, it was only a box; maybe it needed a more specific wish before it could act.

"Gleaming Bright, please, please, turn these statues back into stone." Och, no, they already were stone! "Into useless, lifeless stone!"

A second hard hand closed with painful force about her arm, dragging her back—

But suddenly the terrible force stopped. The hand clamped on her arm shuddered, then fell away, and a second later, so did the one holding her fingers prisoner. Rubbing her sore hand, Finola glanced wildly from one statue to the other as they swayed, then crumbled and fell into two broken mounds of stone.

"Y-you did it," she breathed in disbelief, then hastily bent and scooped up Gleaming Bright, making sure the lid was securely shut. For all she knew, she'd just used up all the power stored within it: she didn't dare waste the chance she'd been given. Fiain—if it had been Fiain—was nowhere to be seen, but deep within the fortress's darkness, more stone slowly groaned and surged.

The rest of the statues are coming to life!

"Run!" a small voice suddenly shrieked in her ear, making her start. "Aie, run!"

It was surely her unknown benefactor, the one who'd warned her not to look behind her, but Finola hardly needed a warning this time. Clutching Gleaming Bright to her, she dashed out the open gateway—only to be hit full in the face by daylight, dazzling her darkness-adjusted eyes. Finola frantically blinked, struggling to clear her vision. There, now she could see a little and—

"Oh gods, no!"

The two horrible stone things guarding either side of the gateway were lifeless no longer. Their stone eyes burning with rage, they swiped down at her with their huge, heavy paws.

No, oh no, not them, too!

She threw herself to one side, not quite in time. Hard, rough stone struck the girl a glancing blow, hurling her off her feet. Finola hit the ground with a jolt that knocked the breath from her, Gleaming Bright digging painfully into her side. Gasping, Finola tried to scramble up, then threw herself flat again as a second stone paw lunged down, snagging briefly in her cloak, nearly strangling her before it pulled free. Wriggling Gleaming Bright out from under her, Finola managed to work open the lid a crack.

"Gleaming Bright, I didn't mean to call on you

again, not so soon, but you've got to stop these monsters, too! Oh, hurry, turn them to rubble!"

But nothing happened, not the faintest spark of magic. As Finola stared up in horror, the monstrous statues raised their paws again. And this time, she knew, they would crush the life from her.

SIXTEEN

Hunter and Hunted

"GLEAMING BRIGHT!" FINOLA SHRIEKED.

There wasn't the faintest spark of magic. The princess twisted aside, gasping, as a stone paw swiped at her. Her father had warned her the box was unpredictable. Maybe she really *had* used up all its power already. Or maybe it just didn't want to answer her!

But why does it have to happen now?

Still, deep below the level of panic, her mind was continuing to work. These stone monsters weren't truly alive, after all; they couldn't really think. Therefore, there must be a regular pattern to the way they lashed out, if only she could find it before they crushed her—

Yes, oh yes, there it was, this paw came down when that paw went up and . . .

Now!

Finola leaped to her feet, ducking this way and that in a hasty dance, the swiping paws just missing her each time. Oh, please, let the things be too heavy and slow to follow her! Ha, yes, they were fixed to their pedestals and couldn't tear free no matter how they raged!

But then a monstrous roar of alarm like the fury of the earth itself thundered out, echoing throughout the fortress.

If that *doesn't wake Rhegeth, nothing will!* Finola thought, and ran with all her might.

Gods, she hadn't realized how far it was to the forest! Gasping, the princess searched frantically for a flash of white amid the darkness. Her lungs were aching; her bruised body seemed one big ache; and—and she couldn't seem to find the stag anywhere!

"Finola, over here!" a familiar voice called. "I'm here!"

With one last burst of speed, she raced to the stag, nearly collapsing against his sleek white side, clinging to him for support. "I . . . have it . . . Gleaming Bright."

"Never mind that now! He's coming!"

Finola glanced wildly back over her shoulder and groaned. Rhegeth was storming down out of the fortress on a great horned beast like a living bolt of darkness, a spear of black fire in the Dark Druid's hand. It would seem that Rhegeth couldn't cast his sorceries from too far away. Or else, Finola thought despairingly, he just enjoyed the thrill of the hunt. "I—I can't run anymore."

"You must!"

"No . . . no . . . impossible." Suddenly inspired, Finola asked, "Stag, please, let me ride you."

"What!"

"You're tall as a horse—Please!"

Reluctantly, he let her struggle up onto his back, staggering a moment under the unaccustomed weight of a rider. Then he gathered himself and sprang off like an arrow from a bow, almost losing Finola right from the start. His gallop was strange, more a series of great bounds than the steady four-beat gait of a horse, and the princess bent low over his gleaming neck, struggling to stay on the sleek white hide and to catch her breath, clinging desperately to stag and Gleaming Bright both. Ha, yes, now she had the pattern of leap and land and leap puzzled out. Catching her balance, Finola dared look back over her shoulder.

"Oh stag, he's gaining!"

Of course he was. The stag was only flesh and blood; he couldn't outrun sorcery.

"Gleaming Bright," Finola gasped, "listen to me." *Oh please, let there be some power left to it!* "If you don't want to go back to darkness, you've got to help us."

She flung open the lid and found—

A twig? We're supposed to use a dried-up little twig to stop a sorcerer?

Maybe its fall had damaged the box after all.

Maybe she really had used up its magic back in the fortress. Maybe . . . Och, what difference did it make? The box had failed them, and Finola tossed the twig away over her shoulder in despair.

A sudden sharp creaking and cracking made her glance back again. "Dear gods!"

The stag rolled an eye back. "What is it?"

"The trees! They're *moving,* they're actually moving. . . . Oh, I see it! They're pulling together into a—a solid wooden wall! Rhegeth is never going to get through that!"

"He's a sorcerer," the stag said shortly. "He will. Eventually." The stag slowed from a full run to a trot to a walk, and at last staggered to a stop. "Danger or no," he admitted wearily, "I must rest."

Rest. What a wonderful thought. "Poor stag, yes." Finola slid from his back, nearly collapsing in a heap, wincing at her aching muscles. Should she try rubbing the stag down as she would a horse? "Was I too heavy a burden?" the princess asked warily.

"Och, no." The stag touched her cheek briefly with his nose. "Hardly a burden at all. It was a strange thing, a rider on my back, but nothing I couldn't bear." He shook himself vigorously, nose to tail, then pawed amid the decaying vegetation till he'd found a few limp strands of green. "Pah. They taste terrible. The sooner we are back in healthy forest, the sooner I will—" His head shot up. "Ah. So soon."

"What—"

But before Finola could finish, harsh, terrible Words of Power shook the forest. The wall of trees trembled, then exploded into dazzling black flame. The stag sighed.

"I knew he wouldn't surrender so easily. Come, Finola."

With a groan, she climbed back onto his back. The stag burst forward once more, weaving his surefooted way down the narrow forest paths. Finola, struggling once more to stay on his back, frantically twisted out of the way of tree trunks that would have crushed her legs, branches that would have cracked her skull. This couldn't be the way they'd come; they were already nearly back into healthy, living forest.

Maybe that will slow Rhegeth?

But leaving his realm didn't seem to be bothering the Dark Druid at all. Finola didn't dare glance back, not lest she get knocked off the stag by a branch, but she could hear, alarmingly close, the fierce breathing of Rhegeth's sorcerous mount. She could also hear the stag's increasingly labored panting and feel the heaving of his sides.

I have to buy him more time to rest! "Gleaming Bright, that twig was all well and good, but it wasn't enough. Come now, a great wizard created you! Surely you can do more to help us!"

Had she insulted whatever sentience the box possessed? For a long time it remained stubbornly empty, so long a time that Finola wanted to weep. But when she flung open the box one last, desper-

ate time, she found that Gleaming Bright con-
tained something after all: one small, sharp thorn.

*Cathbad must truly have had a weird sense of hu-
mor,* Finola thought wearily. *Eh well, let's see what
happens.* Hardly daring to hope, she threw the
thorn back over her shoulder.

But then she saw that the thorn was sparking,
and gave a laugh of wild delight. "Stag, look back!
All those ugly thornbushes that tried to eat us on
the way in are moving."

"Oh, wonderful."

"No, no, you don't understand! They're twisting
themselves into one big barricade behind us. Ha,
yes, a barricade studded with all those nice, knife-
sharp thorns! Let's see him get through *that!*"

"He will," the stag muttered, and kept running.

And all too soon, harsh Words of Power shook
the forest. Finola glanced back to see the last of
the bushes crumbling into black ash, and groaned.
"Did you have to be right?"

"So it seems," the stag said.

By now, they were fully surrounded by living
green and the wonderful, spicy-sweet scents of
healthy growth. But the stag's pace was growing
rougher and slower with every stride, and the
sound of his labored breathing seemed to roar in
Finola's ears.

He can't possibly go on like this. He has to rest!

"Stag, I—I'm getting down."

"Don't . . . be . . . ridiculous. Not . . .
safe . . ."

"It's all right. I have Gleaming Bright to defend me—"

"With what? Thorns? Twigs? Stay . . . with me."

Finola glanced back and gasped. Rhegeth was so close she could see the hard lines of his face, and the wild eyes of his sword-horned mount, a clear, startling blue against so much darkness.

"All right, Gleaming Bright," she cried, "no more cute tricks. This is it: Do you or do you not want to escape?"

How could a box possibly understand her? When Finola cast open the lid, all she found was a small vial of water. *Ah no, what good is* that?

Despairing, she pulled it open and, as she'd done with twig and thorn, hurled it back over her shoulder.

And the world shook. The stag stumbled, nearly falling to his knees. Finola tumbled from his back, landing on her feet with a shock, struggling to keep her balance as the ground groaned and stirred beneath her and leaves and bits of twig rained down on her.

Slowly the earth stilled. A wary bird tried a chirp, then a second. Finola brushed disheveled hair back from her face to see: "Stag, look at that, *look!*"

The stag stared as though turned to stone. "Amazing," he gasped at last, and then again, "amazing."

Finola found she was stroking Gleaming Bright as though it was a living thing, and hastily stopped. Gods, she'd never dreamed she could be holding so much raw Power! And she'd yelled at it as though it was a naughty pup! Handling the little box gingerly, the princess murmured to it, "I'm not going to belittle *you* again. I—I don't even know if I'll ever have the courage to *use* you again!"

For Gleaming Bright had changed the entire shape of the land for them. The flat expanse of dead forest was gone as though it had never been, and in its place glinted the smooth blue surface of a vast lake.

"I . . . don't think he'll be able to get past *that*," Finola said after a moment. "Stag, I—stag?"

The stag had slowly lowered himself to the ground. Stretched out flat like an exhausted fawn, he had already fallen sound asleep. As she watched him, Finola felt a surge of her own exhaustion sweep over her. Why shouldn't she snatch some rest for herself? Surely they were safe now. Wrapping herself as best she could in her tattered cloak, Finola lay down beside the stag, wincing a bit as her bruises complained.

But now, perversely, her mind had become far too busy to let her rest. Gleaming Bright. What *was* Gleaming Bright? Sometimes powerful, sometimes empty—She wouldn't dare come to depend on it, not chaotic as it was. She would never know when it would deign to answer, or how. Which was probably what Cathbad had had in mind. *I don't think Cathbad would have given*

Grandfather Donal anything that could hurt him. But then, who knows what a wizard thinks harmless?

Finola shuddered, remembering how the stone statues had shattered. And . . . Fiain. Had that actually been—No, no, that was impossible; he couldn't possibly have made it to the fortress before them. Or could he?

No. It all must have been illusion—Wait, that didn't make sense, either. How could Rhegeth possibly have known about Fiain and herself? Yet he never could have created an illusion of the outlaw unless he'd actually seen and spoken to the man.

He can't really be trapped in there, can he? Gods, not in one of the statues, or—or . . .

Och, it was all too much to bear right now. The day had been so strange, so terrifying she would have loved to weep over it had she the energy. But the warmth of the stag's body was stealing through her, wonderfully comforting, soothing body and mind together.

Nestled against the stag's sleek white side, too drained to do anything else, Finola fell smoothly into a deep pool of sleep.

❧

Someone was pulling at her. Someone was screeching in her ear, "Wake, wake, danger, wake!"

The voice was so familiar. . . . Ah yes, this must be her mysterious little benefactor again. But why did he have to shout like—

He? He *who?* Finola forced open eyelids that seemed far too heavy to move and blinked up in confusion at a small, scrawny, black-furred creature dancing up and down in a wild frenzy of alarm.

"Get up!" it shrilled. "Get up, get up!"

"Stag, look. The . . . ah . . . child we saved!"

But the stag slept on, never stirring even when Finola shook him. The little black-furred being insisted impatiently: "No child! No child! I am Echi! Hurry, get up, run!"

"Stag, wake up!" Finola cried. "Oh, please, wake up!"

"Too late," said a deep voice.

Finola scrambled to her feet, nearly falling in her hurry to turn and face—

No, ah, no . . .

Rhegeth stood before them, wrapped in his black, hooded robes, a living column of night amid the daylight.

They were trapped.

SEVENTEEN

Confrontations

TO FINOLA'S HORRIFIED EMBARRASSMENT, she heard herself asking inanely, "How did you get past the lake?"

Oh, idiot, how do you think he did? He's a sorcerer; he used magic, of course!

Rhegeth stared at her as though she was an unpleasant little insect, his eyes glinting coldly from under his dark hood. "So this is the thief. Interesting that the sleep-spell didn't hold her." His voice was hardly what Finola had expected: quite calm, quite human. It didn't sound like the voice of an ageless, terrible sorcerer at all.

"I'm no thief," the princess began in nervous defiance, not knowing what else to say.

But Rhegeth continued, unheeding: "Smaller than I'd imagined. And a girl. That, I most certainly had not dreamed. A thief, nevertheless."

"I told you, I am not a thief!"

The Dark Druid looked directly at her for the first time, and Finola licked her dry lips. She couldn't really see his face, hidden as it was beneath that hood, but there was no disguising the eerie power glittering in his eyes. "The box was taken from me," he told her shortly. "I wish it back. Now."

Gleaming Bright! She'd left it lying on the ground behind her! *"You're* the thief, not me!" Finola snapped, trying to keep him from noticing it, thinking, *Oh, wonderful, shout at a sorcerer. Very clever.* But now there was nothing she could do but continue, with a boldness she certainly wasn't feeling, "You stole it from its rightful owner. I intend to return it!"

"Do you?" Rhegeth murmured. "To whom, I wonder?"

"That's none of your—"

"How odd, that such an insignificant little girl-thief should have convinced the box to perform its magic for her. Perhaps, then, she is not so insignificant after all? Perhaps she's even a descendant of that fool Donal?"

"He wasn't a—" Finola clamped her mouth shut. No use giving Rhegeth more information than he'd already puzzled out.

Too late. The Dark Druid was smiling thinly, the smile of someone who has just been given an unexpected gift. "Donal had only the one child," he said softly, "a son. And that son in turn had only the one child: a daughter. And if I am not mistaken, that is who I face, none other than Donal's princess-granddaughter." His bow was perfectly gracious and perfectly mocking.

"And I'm facing Rhegeth, the Dark Druid," Finola replied with her own formal little dip of the head, trying to let good manners buy her a bit of time, edging ever so slightly backwards towards Gleaming Bright.

She wasn't quite subtle enough. Rhegeth's eyes glinted coldly, gaze flicking from her to the box and back again, and raised a hand for what she was sure was a spell.

But before the sorcerer could utter a word, there was a wild thrashing to Finola's left. She shot a hasty glance that way and saw the stag struggling to his feet, head down, plainly trying to fight off the influence of the sleep-spell. Sweat gleamed on his white sides, and he trembled with visible terror, but all at once he seemed to gather his strength together and charged the Dark Druid with a roar of pure fury.

Rhegeth never flinched. "Clown," he said contemptuously, "you should not have returned," and hurled his spear of dark fire. Horrified, Finola saw it strike, saw the stag enveloped in a sudden blinding burst of darkness. It vanished just as swiftly, showing him lying in a crumpled heap.

"No!" Finola screamed.

But before she could rush to the stag's side, the Dark Druid spat out a Word of Power that seemed to turn her legs to stone.

"Forget that fool," Rhegeth crooned. "He still lives."

Finola struggled so fiercely against the spell binding her legs she nearly toppled over. "Let me go!"

"Ah, but my dear young princess, you can hardly expect me to surrender such a prize as yourself."

"What do you—"

"Come now, I doubt you're as foolish as your antlered friend there. You are a girl of the direct royal line, the heir to the throne, she who can coax Gleaming Bright into releasing its magic. I've struggled too long to gain control of that magic to give it up now. No, my dear young woman, I shall use the power of Gleaming Bright through you."

"You will not!" Finola snapped, even though she knew it was empty defiance.

Rhegeth knew it, too. His sudden smile was almost charming. "Come, my dear, it shall not be such a terrible fate. You are already a princess; you must know something of how intoxicating a lure political power can be. No? Are you too young to have realized that? You will learn. You will learn, too, that sorcerous power is even more wonderful." He chuckled. "Here I wondered at my dreams. The dreams I had all the while you were stealing the box away from me." Rhegeth's voice hardened. "The dreams that you and I together shall make real."

"I d-don't know what you're talking about."

"Think now: what if Gleaming Bright's power

was mingled with my own? Ah no, don't interrupt me, rude child. Use your imagination. Picture yourself at my side. With Gleaming Bright's aid, you shall be the mate not of some petty king but of a true ruler of the mightiest realm ever created."

"That's the most ridiculous thing—"

"Hush, child. Watch. Learn."

And the world swung into a wild swirling all about Finola. She gasped, grasping wildly out at nothing, trying to find *up* or *down* or—

Suddenly there was solidity about her once more, a dimly lit stone-walled room furnished in strange, dark wood, a room she felt she must know, a room that surely should be familiar, and yet wasn't . . . quite . . .

Finola blinked in confusion, rubbing a hand over her eyes. What a strange, strange dream . . . wandering in the forest with . . . with only a beast for company . . . a beast. . . . She couldn't remember what type of animal . . . or why she'd been wandering so far from home. . . .

"My dear?" a deep voice asked. "Are you all right?"

For a moment she stared blankly at the man seated across from her. He was older than she by a good many years, or so she thought, and dressed in an elegantly cut robe of soft black velvet. The lines of his face were sharply chiseled, almost cold, and yet not really unhandsome, while his eyes . . .

His eyes . . .

"What—what happened?" Finola asked weakly.

"Don't you remember?" Concern rich in his voice, the man reached out a hand to gently touch her own. "I feared this might happen. We were working a spell together. I feared your memory might be overwhelmed; you are not as used to magic as I. But you insisted, and I . . . och, I agreed."

"We . . . were working a spell . . . ?"

"Yes, my dear. You and I, with the aid of Gleaming Bright. We were casting an enchantment to help our people. See?"

He pulled her gently to her feet, leading her to the room's one window, pulling back the dark, heavy draperies. Finola leaned on the sill, staring out at fertile fields stretching to the horizon, their smooth greenness broken here and there by outcroppings of villages all of dark stone worked finer than any she'd ever seen.

But that wasn't right . . . of course she'd seen this view before. All this was familiar . . . her home . . . and the man worrying over her was . . . was Rhegeth. Yes, Rhegeth, her husband, her loving, gentle husband. . . .

This can't be right. Can it?

"You see, my dear?" Rhegeth was insisting. "This is our home, our realm over which we both rule. You and I together, happy, secure, powerful. This is reality. Accept it. Accept. You are mine, you and Gleaming Bright are mine. Accept."

Why was he staring at her like this? His eyes were so strange . . . so powerful. . . . Finola moaned in confusion and turned away. A glint of color outside caught her vague gaze. Sunlight. Sunlight catching an ornamental pool, turning the water for a moment to a blaze of white—

White. White as snow, her mind murmured foolishly, white as moonlight, white as milk, white as . . . as . . .

As the hide of a stag. Now, why should she think of anything so strange as a stag, a stag . . . a . . . stag?

The stag! Yes, yes, dear gods, of course, the *stag* was the reality, not all this, the stag and Gleaming Bright—

"It's a lie!" Finola screamed.

"Hush, my dear."

"I won't hush! All this is a lie—and I won't believe it!"

"You are overwrought. Come, look at me. Look into my eyes, Finola. See—"

She didn't dare look. "Give it up, Rhegeth!" Finola snapped, as fiercely as she could, refusing to let his soft, sorcerous mist settle over her again. "You won't win, I won't let you win, so you can drop all this pretty illusion!"

"What a clever child," he murmured, almost in admiration. With a wave of his hand, illusion swirled out of being. "What a pity," the Dark Druid added softly, "I must destroy you as you are, change your will and mind forever. But then, who knows? You may still come to like living in my fortress. You may even come to enjoy the darkness."

Finola staggered as the world came sharply back into its rightful shape. To her horror, she saw that during the bewilderment he'd cast on her, Rhegeth had had time to catch up Gleaming Bright. Now he clutched the box under one arm. Och, if only she could reach it! But her legs still wouldn't move.

"I'm sorry, my dear," the Dark Druid said with smooth insincerity, and began a new spell. Finola tried to cover her ears, but that was useless. The soft, sly Words slid past mere physical hearing. They stole their way into her mind like so much cold mist, the Words that would enslave her will forever. . . .

A shrill screech rent the air. "No, no, no, this is wrong, this is not to be!" shrieked a small, black-furred blur: Echi, realizing that Finola was stunned by the sudden rending of the spell.

Rhegeth was even more stunned, staggering back, eyes wild. "How dare you—" he managed to gasp.

Echi never hesitated. It sprang into Rhegeth's arms before the Dark Druid could react and flung back the man's hood. As the sunlight hit Rhegeth fully in his eyes—eyes unaccustomed to light—he cried out in startled pain, flinging up an arm over his face—and sending Gleaming Bright flying.

I can't let it crash down, not again! Finola thought, and threw herself after it, snatching it in midair, hitting the ground herself with breathless force.

"You little fool!" Rhegeth roared at her, eyes

watering with his pain. "Now your pet dies!" He shouted out something so raw and harsh it could only be a Death Spell.

"Don't!" Finola screamed. "Don't—please—"

But the wave of Power was swifter than speech, crashing over the stag, leaving him lying terrifyingly still. *No, no, oh dear gods, no!* Tears blinding her, Finola flung open Gleaming Bright in the vague direction of the Dark Druid, sobbing out, "M-may you get what you deserve!"

A blazing silver mist swirled up out of the box so suddenly Finola gasped. She lost her hold on Gleaming Bright, forced to fling an arm over her eyes to shield them. But the box fell open. She heard Rhegeth cry out in shock, and struggled to look into the blinding silver, heart pounding, eyes watering. The Dark Druid was backing away, eyes wide with horror. But what could possibly frighten him? What? Staring with all her might, constantly wiping the tears from her eyes, Finola made out the figure of a shimmery, silvery figure radiant with its own Power . . . Cathbad! This could only be the spirit of Cathbad the wizard himself!

B-but he's dead!

That didn't seem to be bothering him. Had his spirit been lurking in Gleaming Bright all these many years? Finola wondered wildly. Had he returned from the gods knew where to answer her call?

Or was it to settle old scores? He gestured, and Rhegeth froze. Finola couldn't hear anything through the blaze of silver Power, but she saw the

Dark Druid's lips move, first in fury, then in desperate pleading. But Cathbad, unmoved, raised an imperious hand. Rhegeth, struggling against every step, was forced to move slowly forward. When he was close enough Cathbad reached out, enfolding his old enemy and pupil in an unbreakable grasp.

Finola gasped. She saw Rhegeth shrinking from man to boy, a lost, frightened boy nestling gladly in Cathbad's arms—but then the silver mist flared up so fiercely she cried out in pain. There was one quick glimpse of Cathbad looking straight at her, his eyes warm. Then the mist flared up one last time and vanished—

And so did Cathbad and Rhegeth.

I don't believe it. I don't believe I saw . . . whatever I saw.

Och, but what about the stag? Finola scrambled about to where Echi, bewildered, was crouching over the quiet body, keening a sound so raw and painful it could only be the little being's first tears. "This isn't the way things are supposed to go!" it pleaded with Finola. "Make it not-so!"

Sickened with grief, Finola stroked the cold silver coat. "I'm sorry," she whispered. "Oh stag, I'm so sorry."

"It can't be ending like this!" Echi protested. "It can't!"

It pushed into her arms like a frightened child, fur soft as that of a kitten. "Oh my poor little dear," Finola whispered to the small creature. "I'm afraid it is."

EIGHTEEN

Revelations

"CAN'T GIVE UP!" ECHI chittered frantically. "No, no, can't! Pretty box . . ."

Finola stared at the little being. Then, hardly daring to hope, she snatched up Gleaming Bright, hugging it to her. "Please, please, one more wonder. I wish . . . oh, how I wish with all my heart that the stag was alive and happy and himself again!"

For a long, heartrending time nothing happened.

"It's no use," Finola murmured, putting the box down. "Echi, I'm sorry, but Gleaming Bright must have burned itself out fighting Rhegeth."

"No! Not right!"

Finola sighed. "No, I guess it's not. But either the box has no power left, or—or else it doesn't think a stag's life is important enough." *But it is, oh it is!*

Echi squealed in sudden sharp excitement. "Wait, wait, look!"

All at once a soft golden haze, not at all as terrifying as the silver blaze Cathbad had created, had begun seeping out from the box. Slowly it rose to enfold the stag, hiding him from view while Finola and Echi waited tensely. All at once something stirred within the mist, and Echi gave a wondering little cry.

"What?" it asked softly. "What?"

The soft haze faded, dissipating into the air. Where the stag had lain . . .

"No," Finola said in bewilderment. "This can't be right. . . ."

The stag was gone. In his place, a naked young man, pale-skinned and so fair of hair the tangled locks falling about his face were nearly white, was struggling to rise, crying out in bewilderment, falling, clumsy as—as someone suddenly gone from four feet to only two.

He's the one I saw in Gleaming Bright's mirror! Finola realized with a shock. *B-but he was also my stag, or at least I think he was—Who is he? And what?*

He'd made it to his feet now, swaying uncertainly, face wild with confusion. Finola hastily handed him her cloak, politely averting her eyes, and after a moment in which he seemed uncertain of what he was supposed to do with it, the young man hesitantly wrapped the cloak about himself, fumbling as though he wasn't quite used to having fingers. He blinked, staring at her.

"Finola . . . ?"

The voice was definitely that of the stag. "Who . . . ?" Finola began uneasily.

"I am . . . I . . . have a name . . . a human name. . . ." That was said with great wonder. "I am human . . . yes. I am human, and I have a human name . . . if I can only . . . ha, I have it! Niall," he exclaimed in sudden triumph. "My name is Niall."

"But who is Niall?" Finola prodded warily.

"I am. Och, no, that doesn't make sense. . . . If only I could *remember!*" But then life suddenly flared in his brown eyes. "Yes! Now I know: I am Niall, the son of . . . I am Niall, son of King Anlan."

"His younger son!"

"Yes, I . . . think . . . yes. I am."

Bit by bit the confusion was leaving his face. Niall rubbed a hand over his eyes. "This isn't easy. I've been a stag so long . . . it's strange to see the world as a human again: the vision's so very different. And my nose—there was a whole world of odors out there, but now I can only smell the mere edges—Och, never mind the changes, I'm *human* again, human!"

"But you—Prince Niall—everyone said you were dead!"

He glanced down at himself with a wry little grin. "I certainly don't feel dead! What was supposed to have . . . ah . . . killed me?"

Finola shrugged in confusion. "The stories said it was a hunting accident of some sort. Your horse returned without you, and everyone went searching for you, but they couldn't find a trace of—" She stopped short, staring. "Of course they couldn't find you! You weren't dead; you were a stag all this time."

Niall shuddered. "Not through any choice of my own. I . . . I've been an animal so long, my memory's still shaky, but . . . well, I *think* what happened was that I got separated from the rest of my hunting party. Yes, and wound up wandering, scared as a little boy, through all that dead forest. Ha, yes, that must have been when my horse threw me! Can't blame the poor terrified animal."

"You came across Rhegeth, didn't you?"

"Indeed I did." Niall hesitated. "He must have been in the middle of some sorcery or other; I can't remember that part too clearly. The only thing I know for sure is that his ritual involved the sacrifice of a deer." The prince shook his head wryly. "I can almost feel sorry for the man. Here he is, about to perform some terrible spell that's cost him who knows how much care and effort, and all of a sudden a bewildered young idiot comes wandering right into the middle of it and spoils the whole thing."

"What a shame," Finola said drily.

Niall grinned at her. "But you can't blame him for being furious, can you? I tried my best to apologize, knowing better than to get someone who was so obviously a Dark Druid angry at me, but it didn't do a bit of good. He said—well, he said a great many things, ending up with a shout that if I liked deer so well, I should be one!"

"Och."

"Och, indeed." The humor faded from Niall's face. "He took pretty much everything from me, memory, sense of self, everything."

"Except human speech."

"Exactly. He didn't want me to be *too* comfortable as a stag, oh no. So he left me with just enough trace of humanity to keep me forever alone, with none around to hear me or help me. None save you . . ."

His voice trailed off as he studied her, and the faintest, shiest of smiles suddenly brightened his face. Finola felt herself starting to smile foolishly in return, but somehow she couldn't look away, either. *I was right,* she thought in confusion, *he really is quite nice to look at now that he's smiling. . . .*

A sudden groan made them both start.

"Who—"

"I don't believe it!" Finola gasped. "Fiain!"

The man staggered up to them, ragged, filthy, eyes blank and unseeing. "Beast," he murmured. "I was his beast . . . horns . . . wings . . . his beast."

"Oh dear gods. It really was you in the fortress. He turned you into that terrible horned creature he was riding."

"No more," Fiain begged, his voice a whimper. "No more. Let me be myself. Please, let me be myself."

"But you *are*—"

Niall held up a hand. "I'm not so sure he is," he said warily. "I'm beginning to think you'd better ask Gleaming Bright about him."

Puzzled, Finola opened the box one last time. Thinking over the wording carefully, she said, "May Fiain be happy as his true self."

She and Niall both sprang back with startled yelps as Fiain's tall form sagged, dwindled. . . . Where man had been was—

"A weasel!" Finola cried. "Fiain's a—a *weasel!*"

"Well, that explains it!" Niall added sharply. "No wonder he never smelled quite right to me! Yes, and acted the simple, harsh way he did, all lust and hunting greed—He never was human. All along, Fiain was really a weasel!"

The lithe, golden-coated animal stood up on its hind legs for a moment, nose wriggling, scenting the air, and Finola stared to see the white line of a scar crossing its narrow, pointed face. The weasel dropped back to all fours with an odd little chuckling sound of satisfaction. Shaking off bits of entangling human clothing as it went, it slithered off into the forest and was gone.

There was a moment of stunned silence. Then Niall gave a shaken laugh. "The poor beast must have run afoul of Rhegeth as well. I wonder what a weasel could have done to offend the man. Bit him, maybe." The prince paused. "You don't suppose there are still more enchanted creatures wandering about, do you?"

"Oh, I hope not! There are limits to what even

Gleaming Bright can do." Finola bent to pick up the no-longer-Fiain's discarded boots. "At least now you won't have to go barefoot." Rummaging through the rags of the formerly Fiain's clothing, she added, "There isn't much left worth wearing, but it has to be better than just that ragged cloak of mine."

"Never mind. This cloak has served you well."

Once again he was staring at her, once again she was staring back, nervously, shyly. . . .

"Hem!" said a sharp voice. "Ahem!"

"Echi!"

"These human emotions you two show are well and good," the little being said sharply, and a hint of pain glinted in its bright eyes. "Well and good for humanfolk. But what of me? *I* am not enchanted. I am as I am, the only one of me there is. What *of* me?"

"What do you mean?" Finola asked. "You're free to go—"

"Go where?" Echi asked plaintively. "Tell me where? What is to become of me? I have no place now, no home. I—I would not return to the dark place, the fortress, even if I could."

Ah, the poor lonesome thing! Finola thought. *I don't know what it really is; I don't think I'll ever know. But I can guess it—Echi—had a harsh life with Rhegeth! And Echi saved my life more than once . . .*

So be it. "You can have a home with me," Finola promised, and smiled at Echi's whoop of joy.

"And what of me?" Niall asked hesitantly.

Finola paused a long while, suddenly very unsure

of herself. As stag and girl they had come to like each other very much, maybe even to love each other. But now things were very different, weren't they?

It's going to take time to rethink everything.

And yet . . . underneath, no matter what outer shape he'd worn, the basic essence that was *Niall* always had been there.

"Well now," Finola said sharply, "first you have got to let your poor father know you're alive!"

"Oh, of course."

"And I must take Gleaming Bright safely to my father. I . . . don't think it will work again for me," Finola added sadly, "not after all the times I've used it in quick succession. But it should allow my father to discourage King Conal of Lerlais—"

"Ah, you've been having trouble with him, too," Niall murmured. "So did—and presumably still does—my father." He raised an eyebrow. "Well now, our two lands together should be able to put him in his place once and for all, and I don't even think we'll need Gleaming Bright to help us. And after that . . ." The prince paused uncertainly. "After that," he began again, "after we've settled our respective business . . ."

"Yes?"

"Will . . . uh . . . will you let me visit you? I mean, we . . . uh . . . got to know each other as friends as stag and human. I . . . ." His fair skin reddened. "I'd like to learn to know you as human to human. And I . . . hope you feel the same way."

"As friends?"

He blushed even more. "Or—or whatever happens. If that's all right with you?"

Finola smiled, letting the nightmare of What Might Have Been fade away. "Perhaps," she said. "Och, but how do we *get* home?"

Niall hesitated, head back as though sniffing the air, then stopped, blushing. "I forgot. That isn't going to do me any good anymore. But I *think* I remember enough of how the forest lies. . . . Yes. Let me just scout out the land a bit and . . ." He disappeared into the underbrush. After a moment, his triumphant laugh trailed back to the princess. "Finola, hurry. You're not going to believe where we've come out."

Echi at her side, she pushed her way through a mass of bushes. "A road! Niall, this is the trading road that leads to Irwain! The stories weren't true; I didn't have to reach Rhegeth by going west all that way. I could have gone this way and cut the journey more than in half and—and never have met you," she added more slowly. "Och, well, who's to say what the gods have planned."

"To Irwain first, then," Niall said. "Particularly," he added, glancing at Gleaming Bright, "so you can get that pretty, dangerous thing put safely away."

"Oh, gladly!" Finola glanced up. "The weather's nice and warm. And there should be plenty of food to hunt along the way."

"Anything," Niall said with a shudder, "but venison."

Finola burst into laughter. "No venison," she agreed.

Almost of its own accord, her hand slipped into his. Echi dancing lightly before them, Gleaming Bright between them, Finola and Niall turned their steps towards home.

NINETEEN

Afterwards

FINOLA BIT BACK A cry of impatience. Who would have thought she'd have come this far only to be barred from her own city's gates by foolish, nervous guards? "I repeat," she said as simply as though speaking to a very slow child, "I know I look like a ragged beggar. But have you ever heard a beggar speak so finely? Well? Have you? One more time: I tell you, I am none other than the Princess Finola, and this young man with me is Prince Niall of Taliath!"

"They don't believe you," Niall murmured.

"Are we going to have to go back and live in the forest?" Echi chimed in.

"Curse it all," Finola exploded at the stubborn guards, "if *you* don't believe me, send for someone else! Dubhan, maybe, or Odhran—see, I know the names of my father's warriors—ha, or Una! Yes, that's it, send for Una. Now!"

It was a regal shout—and it was obeyed. Soon a guard returned with the woman. Una, blinking in confusion, stared at this wild young apparition for only a moment before screaming, "My baby! My little princess!"

Bursting into tears, pushing the guards out of her way, she clutched Finola to her breast. The princess stayed safe in her warm, moist embrace for a long, wonderful moment, then pulled gently away.

"I think," she murmured to Niall, "we've been accepted."

🐦

King Eamon sprang to his feet so suddenly his chair flew over backwards with a resounding crash. "Finola? . . . Finola!"

He swept her into a hug so fierce it nearly smothered her, then pushed her roughly away. "How dare you run off like that? Frightening me, infuriating the ambassador—"

"The ambassador! Where is he? Did he—"

"He left in some outrage, I assure you! Oh, I tried to give him some credible explanation—but I had none! Where were you?" he roared. "By all the gods, girl, I should lock you away—"

"Father, please, what of King Conal?"

"I have yet to hear back from him, but the gods only know what he'll do! What were you thinking, Finola? Running off like a—a—I thought you were wiser than that! What were you thinking?"

Finola winced. "I know words aren't enough, but I'm truly sorry I frightened you. But there wasn't much choice about it."

"Sorry! You say you're *sorry!* You're right, words aren't enough! *Where were you?*"

"Hunting," the princess said simply. "See what a prize I've won."

And Gleaming Bright's light radiated gloriously throughout the hall.

❧

Ah gods, it felt so good to be *clean!* Even after a month, Finola still couldn't take for granted the joys of having nice, sleek hair again, or soft, pretty clothes.

And then there was Niall. . . . The princess glanced down from her window to the garden where he played with little Echi, the two of them laughing together. Niall never would be conventionally handsome, Finola thought, but that really didn't matter. Dressed in good, fresh clothing as he was, his near-white hair flying in the breeze as he chased the little creature with something of the stag's easy grace, he made a fine, happy picture. And somehow he made Finola's breath catch in her throat.

Feeling her gaze on him, Niall glanced up. Laughing, he swept down in a courtly bow, fully at home in his body once more. And: *Yes,* a small voice said, deep within her, *oh yes.*

Odd. What she felt wasn't a girl's mere whim. It was a quiet certainty. Finola shivered, not quite in fear, because in this past month matters had been like this, with quick glimpses of possibilities, with strange little knowledges of things she couldn't have known by ordinary means.

Gleaming Bright, she thought in uneasy wonder. *I used it so often in so short a time for such a vast amount of magic that . . . well . . . maybe just a touch of it rubbed off on me.*

But what would Niall think of such a thing? He'd seen so much of magic, good and foul, in such a short time! But she knew, with that same odd little certainty, that her newfound abilities, whatever they might turn out to finally be, wouldn't bother him at all. Ah, Niall . . .

Eh well, there would be time enough for—for whatever eventually. Her father had sent off messenger birds to Niall's royal father, of course, telling him the joyous news, but sooner or later Niall was going to have to go home.

But he will return. Finola smiled at her certainty. *He will return.*

"My princess?" a servant said nervously. "You . . . uh . . . are wanted in your father's hall."

⁊❧

King Eamon sat alone, just as he had so long ago when he'd first told her about Gleaming Bright. The box was nowhere to be seen; when Finola had told him of its strange, chaotic power, he'd locked it safely away.

"Father?"

"I've heard from King Conal," he said shortly. "Who is on his way to us. He *says* he wishes to join in the search for you."

"I see." Finola supposed she should be frightened. Instead, all she felt was a quiet strength stealing through her, almost as though Gleaming Bright were transferring something of its golden glow into her. "Father, you'll excuse me."

"Now where do you think you're going?"

"To talk with Conal," Finola said, and was out the door before he could stop her.

&

King Conal came riding along in glittering splendor, blazing red-and-gold cloak flapping back from a bright blue, gold-encrusted tunic under which glinted a hint of mail. He was handsome as a golden eagle. Splendid, too, was the armor of the warriors who rode with him: not quite enough of them to show out-and-out threat, but decidedly more than would be needed in a simple search.

Finola moved to stop them.

King Conal hastily reined in his horse, signaling to his men to stop. "Finola . . . ?" he asked doubtfully. "Princess Finola . . . ?"

"I am."

"So-o! I'd heard you were lost."

"No longer."

His smile was dazzling. "I am truly glad to hear it. I thought, foolish thing, that you'd run away rather than wed with me."

"No. But I will not wed you."

Conal's smile thinned a touch. "Och, Finola, do you still remember our first meeting? Surely you're old enough now to know a man . . . is a man.

ou've grown into a fine young woman. And when we are wed—"

"I told you. I will not wed you." Finola stared up at his blond elegance, and something deep within her seemed to laugh in sudden wild relief. After all she'd undergone to win Gleaming Bright and free Niall and Fiain, this cold, shallow, *nasty* man no longer produced the smallest trace of fear in her. "Don't bluster, Conal of Lerlais. Look at me. Look."

She felt the power well up within her, calm and determined. "You will go home, Conal of Lerlais. You will give up any thought of wedding me *or* harming my land."

Staring helplessly at her, he tried to argue, to bluster. But Finola, feeling her power radiating from her, saw a spark of bewildered terror flicker into life in his eyes. All at once King Conal turned his horse sharply aside. Without another word, he rode away, his bewildered warriors following meekly behind. Finola stood rigidly watching till they were out of sight, then sank to her knees, shaking, fighting back tears.

"Oh, don't!" cried a familiar voice. Warm arms encircled her.

"N-Niall. You followed me."

"Of course I did. This is the only convenient road from Lerlais, and I suspected this had to be where you were headed so fiercely." The prince grinned. "Echi thought so, too. The little creature wanted to come with me, but I—well, I wanted to be here for you. Alone."

"Niall, I—I—frightened Conal away."

"So I saw!" the prince said cheerfully. "And nicely done, too!"

"But you don't understand! I looked at him and told him to go, and I *frightened him away!*"

"We just established that."

"But I—he—"

"Well now," Niall added, cutting through her stammerings, "I never thought I'd be falling in love with a budding wizard. But then, I never thought I'd be stuck for a time as a stag, either!"

"Love . . . ?" Finola said uncertainly.

"Now what do you think?" The prince pulled her lightly to her feet. "My dear Finola, I've had enough time as my human self again to study how I felt. You were right, back when I was a stag, to call me jealous. I *was* jealous of Fiain, even though as an animal I wasn't quite sure why. What I've come to realize as a human is that I simply don't want to spend the rest of my life without you. And I—I certainly hope you feel the same way."

"I . . . uh . . . yes. Yes."

"Well, good!" the prince exclaimed in relief. "I'm glad that's settled!" For a moment more Niall held Finola fast in the circle of his arms, then released her with obvious reluctance.

I'm reluctant, too, Finola thought, but didn't quite have the courage to say that aloud.

"I wonder," Niall said suddenly, "where the magic's coming from."

"*You* wonder! I—I guess Cathbad transferred a

of his power to me when he looked at me. just before carrying off Rhegeth, I mean."

"Or else," Niall added with a grin, "Gleaming Bright decided it *really* likes you!" Finola gave a shaky laugh at that, and the prince continued thoughtfully, "I suspect you're going to be studying some odd subjects with your father's druids now."

"I g-guess I am. Assuming there's enough power in me to be trained. Assuming it just doesn't drain away again. Assuming—I don't know—Niall, it— all this magic doesn't frighten you?"

"Finola, my dear, brave, confused Finola, the only thing that frightens me is the thought of not seeing you again. Ha, or that I might someday wake up with antlers and a mad craving for salad!"

Finola erupted into laughter. Niall chuckled, then broke into full laughter with her. Arm in arm, they headed happily back to Irwain and the promise of new joy.